Cape Cod Chips, Wiener Dogs, and Swiping Left

STORIES OF SWEET ROMANCE

DAVID H. HENDRICKSON

PP
Pentucket
Publishing

Wendy slid into the booth opposite the mysterious Jason with no last name. Chinese. Short, black hair, neatly combed. About her age. Medium height and weight. Moderately handsome.

Not that she paid attention to that sort of thing anymore. Chinese. White. Black. Short. Tall. Homely. Handsome. Alive. Dead.

Didn't matter. All men had been dead to her for a long time now. Romantically, at least. And that most certainly was not what she was here for.

"So," she said, getting right down to the point, "Corporate malfeasance. Ethically bankrupt and outright illegal. You got my attention."

Jason No-Last-Name opened his mouth and then shut it.

PRAISE FOR DAVID H. HENDRICKSON

"A fantastic writer, one of our best working right now." - Dean Wesley Smith, *USA Today* bestselling writer

"David H. Hendrickson is one of my favorite writers."- Kristine Kathryn Rusch, *USA Today* bestselling writer

Cape Cod Chips, Wiener Dogs, and Swiping Left
Stories of Sweet Romance

Contents

<h1 style="text-align:center">Introduction</h1>

CURRENT CONVENTIONAL WISDOM HOLDS THAT writing romance short stories is a loser's game. Reading them is great fun; writing them, not so smart. It made sense back when the dearly departed *Heart's Kiss* magazine was still in business (and showing the good taste to publish my stories). But now? The number of magazines regularly publishing professional-quality romance short stories sits exactly at zero.

Zero. I don't understand it.

Mystery and crime fiction have *Ellery Queen* and *Alfred Hitchcock's*. Science fiction and fantasy have *Isaac Asimov's*, *Fantasy and Science Fiction*, and *Analog*, not to mention a host of great online-only magazines led by *Clarkesworld*. But not romance, the single most popular genre in the universe. Mind boggling, but true. Which means there's not a lot of motivation to write romance short stories these days.

Except for you, kind reader. And that makes all the difference. Ever since, much to my surprise, I wrote my first romance novel, and then to my utter astonishment, it proved far more popular than anything I'd written to that point, I've appreciated the voracious appetite of readers in this wonderful genre.

While too many of them haven't yet gotten the memo that when it comes to fiction size really doesn't matter— romance short stories are great fun, too—you, kind reader, got the memo and are attending this meeting of our imaginations.

And for that I thank you.

As for the rest, notice I said they haven't gotten the memo *yet*. There's still hope for them, and as long as there's hope for them and even more importantly, as long as you're still here reading my tales of happily ever after, I'm going to have a great time writing them.

That's why I latch onto almost every opportunity when a professional editor puts out a call for a romance short story. Most notably, that comes with WMG Publishing's annual *Holiday Spectacular*, but there are others as well. Unless I'm in the middle of some totally uninterruptable project, I try to pounce on those opportunities.

Like a dog attacking a porcupine? Or a moth to the flame? A writing fool unable to stop himself? I think not. More like Pavlov's dog, hearing the ringing bell of an editor's call for a story, sure that something creatively juicy and delicious awaits me.

Your interest in these stories, dear reader, is my reward. As long as your interest remains, I'll keep writing these stories. And having a great time doing it.

—May 28, 2024

Snowbound

Introduction to Snowbound

Not every heroine and hero in a romance needs to be physically perfect, young, and vivacious. Nothing wrong with that. Novel covers almost universally depict a bare-chested guy with a chiseled physique. The kind of body I can only wish I possessed.

(One time while I was out running, a shirtless Adonis passed the other way. Romance novel, cover-model perfect. Good Lord, I thought, if I looked like that, I wouldn't even *own* a shirt.)

But you know, not everyone fits the stereotype of physical perfection. Or is young, bubbling with energy and *joie de vivre.*

I like to write on the boundaries. Sometimes way outside the boundaries.

So when the call went out for a December holiday romance short story, I veered away from young and effervescent characters, men and women whose biggest problem is that they work too hard at their careers. I added a whole lot of years and heartaches to my heroine and hero, then tossed them into a blizzard.

Yeah, a blizzard. Because they didn't already have enough issues to deal with.

Hey, writers often have to treat their characters badly. I plead guilty. But if those characters get their happily ever after—or at least a happy-for-now—then it sure feels worth it.

Snowbound

JOYCE SANDERSON SETTLED IN BEHIND THE WHEEL of her three-year-old blue Hyundai and pulled out of her driveway. By the time she was halfway down the street, only minutes into the seven-hour journey to D.C. and the grandkids, the aromas from the backseat filled the air. All her holiday cooking: apple pie, pecan pie, cherry pie, brownies, and seven different assortments of cookies from gingerbread to oatmeal to chocolate chip. And that didn't count the custard pie, strawberry rhubarb pie, and pumpkin pie in the cooler.

Joyce sipped her maple pecan coffee, another holiday specialty, from her Yeti. It was piping hot, almost too hot. She briefly considered starting an audiobook but decided to wait and savor the upcoming Christmas celebration with her four grandchildren, two with her daughter and son-in-law in one Virginia suburb of D.C. and the other two with her son and daughter-in-law in another. Joyce could all but hear the joyous shrieks of "Grandma!" as the grandkids ranging from four years old to eight raced to hug her, wrapping their arms around her hips and burying their heads against her stomach. She could already feel their excitement as they tore open their presents. That joy made the seven-hour drive—eight if she dilly-dallied at the stops—a piece of cake, no burden at all. And well worth getting up early for so she could pack the car and be on the road by eight.

It had filled her heart with joyful anticipation the day before to bake all the goodies while listening to her favorite Christmas carols. The *great* Christmas carols, of course. The ones that had stood the test of time. "Joy to the World," "Silent Night," and "O Holy Night!" Not the fingernails-on-a-chalkboard, toneless Santa tunes that made her want to run screaming from department stores. Call her old-fashioned—she was, after all, seventy-two with an artificial hip and an artificial knee and the need to color her shoulder-length, jet-black hair every couple weeks to cover the pale white roots—but she could tell the difference between classics and trash.

Unlike a certain deceased ex-husband.

Joyce liked to think of herself, pardon the immodesty, as a classic. A minor one, to be sure, but still someone special, even if the male species hadn't quite caught up to that concept. Seventy-two going on forty-two. She'd retired as a nurse, but she hadn't retired on life. A connoisseur of the arts, she never missed a museum exhibition. She took online history courses and was learning—at seventy-two, going on forty-two—to play the violin. She walked 10,000 steps religiously every day, keeping athletically trim and healthy. She ate her vegetables, kept her cholesterol low, and didn't miss having a man in her life at all.

Not much, at least.

Most men her age had next to nothing to offer—conversations that began and ended with football and their golf scores—while seemingly being interested in only two types of women. "Make me a sandwich" men wanted a cook, maid, and all-around gofer. Not a partner. A slave. The others wanted a woman half their age. Not just seventy-two going on forty-two, but *physically* forty-two. Without those hideous, unsightly wrinkles and pardon me while I gag, ghastly breasts that sagged halfway to the floor. They wanted a *physical* forty-two-year-old who would do a better job of "keeping the lead in the pencil" as Frank had said on his way out the door all those years ago.

In proof that there either was a God—perhaps a woman!—or at least someone in charge of bestowing justice, Frank had died of a heart attack six months later while having sex with the home-wrecker, potentially after having taken a little blue pill. Apparently, after the first six months, the emptyheaded tart had needed help after all keeping lead in Frank's damned pencil.

Not that Joyce was bitter or anything. She hadn't suggested putting on Faithless Frank's tombstone: *I got what I deserved.* She'd thought it, all right. Had mentally engraved every single letter herself.

But she'd moved on. And if men today preferred the female equivalent of "Rudolph the Red-Nosed-Reindeer" to her "Joy to the World," then so be it. Their loss, not hers. She lived a full life and still had what was left of a wonderful family who she'd be seeing soon. They'd celebrate the holiday together, then go into D.C. itself to visit the museums best suited for youngsters. The Museum of Natural History, the Museum of American History, the

Botanical Garden, and perhaps the Air and Space Museum with an IMAX show. Joyce had seen them all multiple times and couldn't wait to see them again.

After a few more sips of the maple pecan coffee, still hot in her Yeti, Joyce pressed the button on her smartphone to start the audiobook of a new lecture series on the history of China's imperial dynasties. She certainly had no need for directions dictated by the smartphone. She'd driven this route so many times, she knew it by heart. How hard was it to remember to follow I-95 in one of its three lanes for the next several hundred miles?

When snow began to fall, Joyce didn't worry. Before retiring to warmer climates, she'd driven for decades in New England. She could handle herself. She knew snow like the back of her wrinkled hand.

She lasted several hours—well into the Tang dynasty—before stopping for gas, use of the restroom, and a fresh cup of hazelnut coffee.

Piece of cake, even with the snow piling up. The plows were out, rumbling noisily along the interstate, sparks flying as metal scraped against pavement. The lectures on the Chinese dynasties continued to be quite fascinating. Joyce stopped for a quick bite to eat—a fast food fish sandwich—and a stop in the ladies' room, then was back out on the road again.

She couldn't wait to see the grandkids. And of course, her son and daughter and their spouses. Just a few hours more.

The snow came harder, and then harder still, the winds blowing it sideways and buffeting the snow-covered

Hyundai. Joyce turned the wipers on maximum speed. *Thwack, thwack, thwack!*

Without realizing it, she leaned forward in her seat. She could see just fine. Night hadn't yet fallen and wouldn't fall before she got to Sheila and Bob's house. But nervous instincts die hard. Joyce's grip on the steering wheel tightened.

She stopped the lecture recording. Not that she really wanted to hear the thumping of the windshield wipers—and her heart—but whatever the lecturer was saying about the Song dynasty was now going in one ear and out the other.

"Nothing in between to stop it," Frank had often said, though by any measure she was the smarter of the two. Better grades. Higher test scores. And enough sense not to leave a good, loving, interesting spouse for a tramp.

Where had that come from?

Joyce shook her head and again tightened her grip on the steering wheel.

Less than two hours to go. So close. Images of the grandkids screaming, "Grandma!" raced through her head.

Joyce passed an exit with a service station and kept going. She had more than enough gas to make it. A quarter of a tank. It wouldn't even be close. She just wanted to get to Sheila and Bob's house. See little Mikey and Julie.

Joyce passed first one exit with lodging and then another. She wasn't stopping. Not this close. No need to lose a day. Still daylight. Only snow, albeit considerable inches piling up. Been there, done that.

Little Mikey and Julie. Their cute smiles. They'd love

the gingerbread cookies. Decorated with red and green icing.

Joyce didn't begin to worry until she hit her first patch of ice. Brief, but unmistakably ice. She slowed considerably even though she'd already been well below the speed limit and in the rightmost lane.

And then a second patch of ice. This time, the Hyundai slid for more than just a second or two. It started to go sideways. Joyce corrected, pointing the nose of the car straight ahead down the road, and though the car fishtailed, it righted itself and then hit solid pavement.

Joyce's heart jackhammered. Her mouth was dry as cotton. Ice was an entirely different question from snow. She could handle snow. She knew snow. But no one could handle ice. She'd take the next exit that promised lodging and stay the night even though it meant a night lost with the grandkids. Better safe than sorry. Better Mikey and Julie get to see their Grammy than have to view her in a funeral home.

The bitter taste of disappointment flooded Joyce's mouth, but she swallowed hard and focused on the road. She moved the car to the middle of the three lanes even though she'd slowed to a crawl. The middle lane was the most traveled and offered the barest pavement. She usually pulled to the right to let faster cars go by, but now was a time to be selfish. And if this forced the other cars to slow down, perhaps she'd be saving a life.

Please, let there be an exit soon. Let there be an exit soon.

A car flew by on the left, honking. Joyce put on her emergency flashers.

The snow, pelting sideways, dropped visibility suddenly to nothing.

Joyce's heart pounded. She leaned forward, desperately trying to stay on the path of the tire tracks before her. She slowed to less than fifteen miles an hour.

Please, let there be an exit.

There was no safe choice. She couldn't stop. She could barely continue.

For an instant, the solid sheet of snow coming down parted enough for her to make out flashing red lights in the distance.

Then she hit ice. The car slid sideways. She corrected for the slide.

Tapped the brakes to slow even more.

And then a wall of cars and trucks materialized in front of her, turned sideways and diagonally. Four lanes wide on the divided three-lane roadway.

Nowhere to go.

Almost slowed to a complete stop, the Hyundai slid until it got to within inches of a black SUV and then stopped. Not quite touching it.

Seconds later, though, Joyce felt the thump of a car behind her drive into the Hyundai. Not a violent crash at all. Not really even a crash. More of a nudge.

Ted Browning sipped his bitter, black coffee, still near-scalding, and gripped the steering wheel. The snow was coming down harder, but the I-95 traffic was thinning and he could still see just fine in the early afternoon light. In fact, he'd put on his sunglasses long ago because of the blinding brightness of the carpet of snow alongside the three lanes heading north.

He sure wasn't stopping now. He'd just topped off the gas tank of his midsize Buick, used the facilities, grabbed the black coffee, and downed half a fast food cowburger that tasted like cardboard before throwing out the rest. A bag of stale donuts rested on the empty passenger seat. Stopping was not an option.

He was going to make it to Fredericksburg, Virginia, even if it killed him. He didn't have a death wish. He'd just never gotten back his life wish.

He'd lost it five years earlier, on this very day, December 21st. Lost it along with Lisa. Cancer, of course. Didn't it always seem to be cancer that claimed the angels?

They'd been married for forty-four years. Had hoped she could make it to forty-five years the next June. So she suffered through more chemo and radiation and experimental treatments than any healthy person could possibly endure, much less someone weakened with terminal illness.

It tore the heart out of Ted to watch. Helpless.

When Lisa clearly wasn't going to make it to their forty-fifth, they scaled back their hopes to one more Valentine's Day together. And then when hope for even that grew bleak, they scaled it back to one more Christmas.

One last Christmas together.

But they didn't even get that.

They got one last December twenty-first. Actually fifty-three percent of the day because Lisa passed at 12:43. Fifty-three percent of the twenty-four hours. Ted had calculated it.

They'd met in Fredericksburg all those years ago, bumping into each other, literally, while viewing one of the city's many historical sites. It had been instant magic for them both. Ted invited her out to dinner, one thing led to another, and a year later they were married.

Forty-four and a half years later, he sprinkled her ashes, per her request, in the Rappahannock River that bordered the city. He returned on her birthday, their anniversary, and December 21st.

It was over eight hundred miles and twelve hours from where he'd retired in Florida—a two-day trip at his age of seventy-three—but it seemed the least he could do. It wasn't as though his life was filled with important appointments anymore. His once-active life as a history professor had evaporated into a whole lot of nothing. Their three children had migrated to the ends of the Earth, Johanna to Austria where she taught music, Stephen to Alaska doing petroleum consulting, and Diane to Silicon Valley working on microprocessor chips for Intel. Only Johanna had had children, a boy and a girl, so Christmas with the grandkids typically meant an awkward Facetime call.

Ted had the distinct feeling that they were all just waiting for him to die. Not in a mean-spirited way. But Lisa had been the glue that held the family together and he had to admit he hadn't exactly been a ray of sunshine to be around since her death.

A dark cloud seemed to hang over his shoulder. He wasn't a total basket case. He *functioned*. He got out of bed every morning, brushed his teeth, combed his pure white hair, trimmed his beard, drank coffee, ate breakfast, read the newspaper, and whiled away the hours doing a whole lot of nothing.

Fake it till you make it, said some experts. Well, he had the faking it down pat now. But he sure wasn't making it. The joy in his life had passed with Lisa.

Ted was going through the motions, and he knew it. And felt helpless to get out of the cycle. The dark storm cloud hanging over him wouldn't go away.

So as the snow now pelted down harder and harder, and the visibility dropped more and more, Ted sipped his bitter black coffee and kept driving. He slowed down—a lot—but it was Fredericksburg or bust. And if fate, coupled with his own damned stubbornness, sent him off the icy roads and into a concrete bridge abutment, there were far greater tragedies in the world.

It was hard to fear death when you'd lost your love for life.

Boo-hoo, he told himself. *Cry like a baby. Waaaah! Woe is me.*

But knowing he was being pathetic didn't empower him to stop it. The dark cloud hovered and wouldn't go away. So Ted cranked up the '70s station on the Buick's satellite radio, grabbed a Boston Cream out of the bag of donuts, and prepared to make the best of it.

When he hit the first patch of ice, his heart leapt into his throat. He slowed to a crawl and moved to the rightmost lane. Visibility was getting really bad. The snow was blowing sideways and even hunched over the steering wheel and with his lights on, it was hard to make out the track of dry pavement.

Then it became hard to make out the cars ahead.

Like the ones suddenly dead ahead. Not moving. Filling not just all three lanes, but the breakdown lane and even angled into the median.

Forming a wall. Unmoving. And with no way around it.

Ted slammed on the brakes. Did nothing but skid. Then remembered to pump the brakes.

He did so, but it was too late. Even at his at-a-crawl rate of speed. The ice was sheer. No traction at all.

He'd almost come to a complete stop when his front bumper crunched lightly into the rear of what looked like a Hyundai. Mostly covered by snow, but with a patch of blue showing.

It hardly qualified as a collision. The two cars barely touched. But they did.

Ted rocked back and forth in his seat. Then saw the glare of headlights coming from behind. An SUV wasn't going any faster than he'd been going, but it still hit the Buick with more than just a touch.

Ted rocked back and forth again.

Another car slid by to his left, right outside his window, then came to a sudden crunching halt.

Ted went to open the door but wondered what was safe. Was anything?

He rolled his window down and poked his head out. Looked behind.

Then heard the blast of an air horn. From a jackknifing eighteen-wheeler sliding his way.

～

Shivering, Joyce stood outside her Hyundai. Snow whipped sideways in the gusting wind, stinging her cheeks. She'd pulled on a jacket she'd stowed on the back seat next to all the goodies, but it was nowhere near thick enough. It had been sixty degrees the day before in Charleston, and though she was going north, it wasn't that far north. She'd never expected anything like this. Nor had she turned the radio on.

Standing beside her was the man from the car that slid into hers. A kindly, good-looking tall man her age with a full head of white hair and a neat, trimmed beard. But a bit too thin, gaunt almost.

"Are you all right?" he asked, concern filling his sad eyes.

"I'm fine," Joyce said. "What about you?"

"I actually got hit harder by the car behind me. I'll have to exchange papers with him, too. But I'm fine."

They exchanged names, then both dove back into their cars for their insurance papers and exchanged that information, too.

"What happened?" Joyce asked, as much to herself as the man, this Ted Browning.

They looked down the road and a sideways gust of wind parted the snow enough for them to briefly see an overturned tractor trailer a hundred yards or more in the distance. Presumably, it had jackknifed, flipped over onto its side, and kicked off a chain reaction. It blocked all three lanes and the breakdown lane to boot. Nothing could get past it. In its wake was a logjam of cars, SUVs, pickup trucks, and another eighteen-wheeler, this one upright. They filled the three snow-covered lanes, all trapped behind the overturned truck.

"What a mess!" Joyce said, as other drivers emerged from their cars and shook their heads.

"I'm not going to make it," Ted said sadly. "I'm going to be late. I should have left earlier. Why didn't I leave earlier? It's going to take forever to clear this. And the snow's coming down harder and harder. I'll never get there tonight."

"Neither will I," Joyce said, fighting back her own disappointment. She brushed snow off her face. "But at least we're safe."

Ted nodded but didn't seem convinced. He brushed snow—or were they tears?—from his eyes. Then he looked behind them at the half dozen cars between them and another jackknifed, though upright, tractor trailer.

"I thought that one was going to wipe us out," he said, pointing to the eighteen-wheeler. "That driver did one heck of a job controlling that rig as much as he did. He might have saved both of our lives."

Joyce nodded, wide-eyed. "Now it's shielding us from more traffic plowing into us."

"Nothing's getting past that bad boy back there," Ted said, "or that one up ahead. We're stuck in the middle and going nowhere."

"A *kaka* sandwich," Joyce said without thinking. She threw a hand up to cover her mouth. "I'm sorry. That was inappropriate."

Ted blinked, then began to laugh. "No, you nailed it. A *kaka* sandwich. And we're the *kaka*."

Joyce breathed a sigh of relief, even though she didn't quite understand why Ted's approval or disapproval meant anything to her. It certainly shouldn't.

She looked around at all the other drivers who poked their heads briefly out to survey the situation, then ducked back inside their cars.

She waited until the silence grew too awkward.

"Well, I suppose we should get back inside our cars and turn on the heat," she said. "No sense freezing out here."

"I guess you're right." Ted wiped snow off his forehead. "Sorry for crashing into you," he said with a pained smile.

"Oh, I wouldn't call it a crash," Joyce said. "It was more like the two cars kissed."

Ted looked at her funny. Joyce felt funny. She'd meant the comment only as a joke, but perhaps her subconscious had more in mind. A Freudian slip, perhaps?

Then he laughed. "Kissed, or perhaps something a lot more rude."

Joyce reddened and suddenly felt hot all over. Embarrassment? Or a pleasant tingle she hadn't felt for so long, she'd almost forgotten what it was like?

TED DRUMMED HIS HANDS ON THE STEERING wheel. Warm air from the idling Buick's heat vents blasted on his face and feet.

What had he been doing with this woman, this Joyce Sanderson?

Perhaps something a lot more rude?

He hadn't intended to embarrass the woman. He'd wanted to make her laugh, the way she'd made him laugh. Laugh like he hadn't in a very long time. Laugh with innocent little quips. Silly quips, really. A *kaka* sandwich. Silly. But funny.

So how had he repaid the debt? By totally overstepping his bounds. Totally! He'd embarrassed the nice woman. *Perhaps something a lot more rude.* He might as well be one of those vulgar comics on HBO.

Shameful, that's what it was. Shameful!

And what was he doing flirting with her in the first place? Because that's what it had been. Flirting! On the anniversary of Lisa's death! An anniversary where he hadn't paid a second's attention to the weather reports, so he wasn't going to get to Fredericksburg on time.

Did it get more shameful than that?

All because this nice woman, Joyce, had made him laugh. Had lifted the dark cloud hovering over him—

Ted's jaw dropped. He blinked rapidly.

Had she really?

She had! For just that short while, the cloud had lifted.

And he'd laughed! Laughed at the *kaka* sandwich. Laughed at their cars kissing. Kissing!

Laughed because the very thought of kissing—

No, he would not go there. Not go there on a sacred anniversary day that he already was defiling by not being where he was supposed to be. Defiling because he was flirting with another woman! Defiling because he was taking that other woman's innocent comment about kissing—at least it had been innocent for her—and becoming so vulgar as to say something as offensive as *perhaps something a lot more rude.*

Disgraceful. The sweet woman deserved better. And

Lisa—at least her memory—deserved better. The whole world deserved better... than what he had to give.

He should go and apologize. He hadn't meant to embarrass with his off-color humor. But what had he expected? This woman wasn't a member of the current generation that was F-this, and F-that, and isn't this an F-ing bleepshow. This was a woman of his generation and his sense of propriety. His kind of a woman.

His kind of a woman?

Was that what he was thinking? On the anniversary of Lisa's death?

Times like these, Ted hated himself. And most times were times like these.

Joyce felt just a bit lightheaded—in a good way— frozen but lightheaded until she started the Hyundai and looked at the gas gauge. Her jaw dropped. The needle wasn't on empty. It was barely below an eighth of a tank.

But it would be hours before crews got cars like hers moving again. It might even be overnight. The overturned tractor trailer might need to be unpacked before it could be righted. As the snow piled up—and it was piling up fast, perhaps eight inches already—and ice patches affected the rescue crews, especially after nightfall and temperatures dropped, rescue times would take longer and longer.

She'd read about cases like this. People would eventually abandon their cars and panicking, try to walk to rescue. Even in the middle of a blizzard—at least that's what this felt like—and the nearest exit miles away. Then abandoned vehicles formed their own logjams, each having to be towed away. Cases like this could take twenty-four hours or more. She'd lived in the Boston area during the famed Blizzard of '78, when cars were stranded on Route 128 for as long as four days.

Though she still was shivering, Joyce turned off the ignition. She had to ration the gas, and therefore, sadly, ration the heat. It would do no good to have help arrive and be sitting here with an empty tank. Even worse, it would do no good to blast the heat now, still well before sundown, and then have none to blast when temperatures plummeted overnight.

Was freezing to death a possibility? She supposed so.

Joyce closed her eyes and cursed her rush to get to the grandkids, delightful as they might be. If only she'd stopped for the night. If only she'd made one extra stop for gas. Heck, if only she'd topped off the gas tank in her previous stop to use the facilities. But no, she'd been in too much of a hurry.

Joyce wrapped her arms around herself for warmth and tried to stop shivering. In twenty minutes, she'd turn the car back on and feel the heat blast all over her.

Twenty minutes.

Nineteen. Shivering.

Eighteen.

At seventeen and a half, she pretended the arms wrapped around her were Ted's. A not entirely proper thought, but a pleasing one nonetheless. She felt warmer already.

Seventeen and—

A wrap sounded on her window.

Joyce sat bolt upright, a scream escaping from her lips.

But couldn't see out the window. It was covered with a layer of snow.

"Who's there?" she called out, pressing the button to open the window a crack. But nothing happened because the car was turned off.

"It's Ted!" came the voice. "From the car that hit you," he added, quite unnecessarily. Joyce needed no reminder. She knew the voice. Had heard it in her overly imaginative mind as she'd pretended the arms wrapped around her were his. Like a silly schoolgirl.

Ted brushed the snow off the window so she could see his face. Slowly, she opened the door a crack.

"What's wrong?" she asked.

"You're going to freeze if you don't turn your car on," Ted said.

"I'll run out of gas," Joyce admitted. "I'm too close to empty. I was in too much of a hurry to stop."

"Come back in my car. I've got a full tank of gas and the heat is blasting. It'll go all night if necessary."

Joyce didn't need any coaxing. Blasting heat sounded wonderful. Heavenly.

Jumping into a stranger's car was not something she'd do under any other circumstances. Not chance, even if she was a pretty good judge of character (Faithless Frank being the exception that proved the rule). But these circumstances were special. And if Ted really was a threat to destroy her faith in all mankind, she'd bring her keychain with the micro-cannister of pepper spray. You could never be too safe.

"I'll be a perfect gentleman," Ted said, as if reading her mind. "And I apologize for my previous risqué remark."

"That will be wonderful! Thank you!" With a coy smile, Joyce added, "And you'll only need to apologize if you fail to repeat the remark."

A MINUTE OR TWO LATER, JOYCE POKED HER HEAD inside the passenger side door. A blast of freezing cold air hit Ted between the eyeballs, but he still smiled and she jumped inside.

She held out a brown paper bag. "Cookies!" she said proudly.

Ted tried valiantly to keep the smile plastered on his face. He didn't really care for cookies at all. Not a single variety. But he couldn't shatter the look of delight on Joyce's face.

"I also brought all kinds of pies on this trip for my son and daughter's families but figure those would be pretty messy to bring in here," she said. "So I left them in the backseat. It's your choice of cookies. Gingerbread, oatmeal raisin, chocolate chip, Swedish toffee—"

"I'll try the Swedish toffee," Ted said, and tried to convey eager anticipation when in reality it was the only one he hadn't ever tried before.

He hated to start off a relationship with a lie or half-truth. Was that what was happening here? Of course, it was! He hated to mislead her, but he just couldn't bear to burst

Joyce's bubble with the truth: "I'm really not a fan of cookies."

So Ted took a bite and though he thought it dreadfully dry and boring, even worse than the other cookies he'd known to dislike, he licked his lips and said, "Delicious!"

Joyce's face fell. "You don't like it?"

"No, I love it," Ted said, "It's delicious." He forced himself to take another bite and smile.

"You are the worst liar I have ever met."

Ted blinked. "I, um..."

"I bet you lose at poker."

"Well..."

"Because it's written all over your face that you do not like the cookie, you're forcing yourself to eat it, and you're only saying it's delicious to make me happy."

"Wow, you're good," Ted said, shoulders slumping.

"Please don't lie to me," Joyce said, looking distressed. "It's a terrible way to start... to start anything. Whatever we're starting here."

"I'm sorry. You just looked so happy, and I couldn't bear to crush that."

"Okay," Joyce said, nodding. "Forget the Swedish toffee cookies. What kind of cookies do you like?"

Ted licked his lips. If honesty was what she wanted—and it was the right foundation for... for whatever they were doing here—then honesty was what she would get.

"I don't like any cookies," he said, cringing. "None of them. Never have. I'm sure yours are the best there are, but I just don't like cookies."

"If I left this entire bag of cookies with you, you'd never eat a single one?"

"Not a single bite."

"Nothing could ever compel you to eat one?"

"I would eat one," Ted said after a moment's thought, "only if I were starving to death in the jungle on *Naked and Afraid*."

Joyce stared at him. Then said, "If you were on *Naked and Afraid*, I'd change the channel."

They stared at each other for long seconds. Then erupted in laughter.

THE HEAT IN TED'S BUICK FELT GLORIOUS AND the conversation was better still. Joyce shared that she'd been a nurse for decades in Boston before retiring. Today, she'd been rushing to get to her grandchildren for the holidays and would be visiting D.C. museums with them afterward. She loved museums, pretty much all the arts, was learning to play the violin, and considered herself quite the U.S. History afficionado.

"Actually, I was a history professor before I retired," Ted said with a grin. "So we may not share a love for cookies, but we sure do share a love for history."

"Oh, my!" Joyce said, embarrassed. "I may be quite a good history student, but you're an expert. Compared to you, I'm just a dilettante."

"And I'm sure you have areas of expertise such as biology and anatomy that overwhelm me in similar fashion," Ted said. "The point is that you have a wonderful brain. You're not just a pretty face."

With those words, Joyce was smitten. Cookies, schmookies. Ted was the real deal.

"So what were you rushing to get to today?" she asked. "You seemed pretty upset you were going to miss it."

Ted was quiet for a very long time.

"This is a lot more difficult to be honest about than cookies," he said. He looked down and his eyes tightened. "Today was the fifth anniversary of my wife Lisa's death. Cancer. A long and painful battle. I always visit Fredericksburg on her birthday, our anniversary, and the anniversary of her death. It's where we met and a river there is where I sprinkled her ashes. She was a special woman. This will be the first time I failed to get there on time."

Joyce let the solemnity of those words hold sway. She said nothing for what felt like a long time.

"A devoted husband," Joyce finally said. "I respect that so much. I wish my own husband, ex-husband, had shown that loyalty."

"He was unfaithful?"

"He left me for a much younger woman. Decades younger."

"He found a younger woman more attractive than you?" Ted asked, looking befuddled. "Really? How? Why?"

Joyce wanted to hug Ted and never let him go. Those were the sweetest questions, honestly asked, ever.

"It had a happy ending of sorts, though," Joyce said. "He died in bed with her."

"Seriously? In bed-bed?" Ted asked, eyebrows raised.

Joyce nodded.

Ted shook his head. "That is a happy ending."

Again they laughed uproariously. It was becoming a habit. A habit Joyce could get used to.

Conflicting emotions crossed Ted's face. He began to speak, then stopped.

"Talk to me, Ted," Joyce said gently, and stroked his hand.

"It may be time for you and Lisa to meet," Ted said, then winced. "That sounded weird, I know. Sorry. But she said many times before she passed that she hoped I would find someone to share the rest of my life with. Not the day after she died or a month after, of course. I should pay my respects to what we had. But life was too short to be wasted. We only have one life to live. All those happy platitudes.

"But I never found anyone I was remotely interested in. Perhaps because I didn't try very hard. Perhaps because I just wasn't ready. Perhaps I just needed to find that special person.

"Well, I'm ready now. And although I barely know you, I already feel quite sure you're a very special person."

"I am," Joyce said, telling herself that she couldn't wait to show him just how special. "And I feel the same way about you."

"So if we ever get out of here," Ted said, "I'd like you to come with me to Fredericksburg and the Rappahannock River. That may seem weird. It's sure not normal. But I'd like to think it will be a passing of the torch from her to you. From the past to the present and future."

THE NEXT DAY, FREED FROM THE NIGHTMARE ON the interstate, Ted and Joyce held hands on the banks of the Rappahannock River. A cold, clean wind whipped at their faces, but not a single snowflake was in sight. They spoke solemn words to the memory of Lisa and solemn words to the promise of a bright future with each other.

When there were no more words to speak, they wrapped their arms around each other and kissed. It was long and slow and sweet. They held on as if for dear life. And they knew there would be many more to come.

No Pity Party

HERE'S ANOTHER WINTER HOLIDAY STORY, THIS time starring two college athletes. As such, they make for, in most ways, an opposite-end-of-the-spectrum contrast with Joyce and Ted in "Snowbound." Nonetheless, JoJo and Derek, the two "No Pity Party" athletes, face steep challenges in their own lives after suffering savage blows to their psyches.

I wrote "No Pity Party" for WMG Publishing's *Holiday Spectacular*, an advent calendar of fiction that is a unique and brilliant source of short stories in the romance, crime, and science fiction/fantasy genres. Sadly, this story was not a fit for the *Spectacular*, but it experienced a happily ever after anyway. Shockingly, Dean Wesley Smith bought the story for his *Pulphouse Fiction Magazine*. I'm honored to have become a mainstay at that legendary magazine, but Dean rarely includes romances in its pages. It's my writing in other genres he's most typically publishing.

Hence, my stunned but exuberant surprise.

I hope you fall for JoJo and Derek as totally as... well... maybe, just maybe.. they fall for each other.

34

No Pity Party

HEAT BLEW SOFTLY DOWN FROM THE OVERHEAD vents in the darkened interior of the somber, almost tomb-like team bus. JoJo Taylor, sitting alone and by the right side window a third of the way back, slipped her fourth slice of pizza out of the now-half-empty, large white box sitting on her lap. Glumly, she bit into it. The crust seemed crunchy and chewy enough, which was how she usually liked it, and the tomato sauce and cheese, though luke-warm, had just the right amount of garlic. Any other time, she'd be enjoying it. She'd have devoured the whole thing in no time, then begun looking around for more.

Inhaled it. That's how she was after games. Ravenous.

Now, though, the pizza tasted like cardboard. She ate it robotically only because her oversized body needed to refuel. Tops on the basketball team in height and weight, she stood six-two with broad, powerful shoulders and the beefy, muscular physique of a weightlifter.

She'd played almost every minute of the Fairview University Falcons' basketball game this afternoon against

Carolina State, a humiliating loss in the consolation round one day after playing almost every minute in an even greater humiliation at the hands of the tournament hosts, Massachusetts State.

Her long, straight brown hair tied back, as always, in a ponytail, JoJo was wearing her white Falcons warmup suit with blue falcons on the back and over the left chest. Until this weekend's Mistletoe Madness tournament, she'd always worn the warmup suit and jersey with pride, win or lose.

Pride, however, was tough to muster after getting destroyed by Mass State in the opener, 104-23, and then by Carolina State, 91-31. The two opponents hadn't just defeated them soundly. They'd robbed them of all dignity. Ripped their hearts out.

104-23.

91-31.

Kicks to the gut. Obliterating whatever pride they'd ever held.

The 104-23 shellacking had been capped off by a Mass State benchwarmer taking a three-point shot (and making it, of course) with a 101-23 lead. Why? Had the point spread been eighty? It had been a benchwarmer, sure, since the regulars had long since settled in on the bench to rest, and maybe she was doing whatever she could to impress the Masshole coach, who was infamous for running up scores and never taking the foot off the pedal. Pedal to the metal for all forty minutes. Foot on the throat.

And then a day later, Carolina State played a trapping defense in the fourth quarter with a fifty-point lead. Creating one turnover followed by an easy layup after another.

Robbed of all dignity.

Even before the first tip-off, no one had given them a chance and for all the obvious reasons. Mass State, Carolina State, and Louisville were all national powerhouses in women's basketball. They all drew close to ten thousand fans a game. Season tickets. Even luxury boxes shared with the men's teams.

Fairview, a small Connecticut school that had only moved up to Division I sports in recent years, drew little more than friends, family, and teenagers let in for free with the hope they'd someday become paying ticketholders. Fairview didn't belong with the big dogs.

They were the Not Ready for Prime Time Players.

Mass State, host of Mistletoe Madness, would reciprocate with the other big-time programs and travel to their tournaments in future years. But not to Fairview's Auld Lang Syne Tournament this New Year's Eve or any other. The Auld Lang Syne would attract only the other nobodies in the sport. For Mistletoe Madness, Fairview was the sacrificial lamb, a deliberate mismatch by the host's design, there to give a rested Mass State team an edge in the championship game. Fairview's athletic director had happily taken the appearance check and prattled on in press releases about how the experience and notoriety were important steps forward for the program.

104-23. 91-31.

Yeah, JoJo thought, *really important* steps forward. Somehow, she'd convinced herself beforehand that the team could perhaps stick with the powerhouses for a half, just be in striking distance, and then see if a miracle could happen. If you couldn't conjure up that belief, you had no chance.

You were defeated before you started. But she might as well have believed in Santa Claus. She'd been a fool. They'd never had a chance.

She couldn't even take any personal satisfaction out of the debacle. At six-two, she was a giant among women, just like the other teams' stars. And strong as an ox. Even stronger than some of them. But the similarity to the other stars ended there. They'd be playing in the WNBA after graduation. They were *athletes*. Quick, skilled, and nimble. *Talented*. She was, she knew now, just... tall. Tall and lumbering.

Both opponents had applied a smothering defense on her, doubling her front and back. And when JoJo had managed to get one-on-one with the other teams' stars, she'd found out why they were headed to the WNBA and she was destined for an accounting firm. They'd throttled her, holding her almost scoreless. She'd gotten almost all her points against the backups, and even they had made her look bad on both offensive and defensive ends of the court. How many of her shots had been blocked this weekend? How many turnovers?

She was a joke.

"Hey."

The softly spoken word startled JoJo. She looked up. It was Makayla, her co-captain though they were both only juniors, carrying a large pizza box. Makayla was only five-four, practically Lilliputian by college basketball standards, but a dynamo of energy. Lightning quick. The Falcons' starting point guard. African American and gay, Makayla had beautiful black hair, cornrows in the front and box braids in the back down past her shoulders.

"Want company?" she asked, but sat down beside JoJo without waiting for a response. She slid the pizza box onto JoJo's lap on top of the one already there. "Four extra slices. Help yourself."

JoJo started to respond that she still had several left only to realize she'd robo-eaten them. She pulled out one of Makayla's slices and bit in.

Cardboard.

"You looked pretty wrecked after the game," Makayla said. "Wanted to make sure you're okay."

"It was pretty tough to take," JoJo admitted. "Never had a beat-down like that. Eighty-one points against the Massholes! Wasn't enough to crush us. Had to take our souls, too."

"Tough to swallow," Makayla said.

"Just really bad timing," JoJo said, and instantly regretted it.

"How so?" Makayla asked, cocking her head. "The holidays?"

JoJo couldn't believe she'd let it slip.

"Your period?" Makayla asked.

JoJo instinctively avoided lying, though it would have been infinitely easier in this case. So she blurted out the truth.

"I had a bad experience at a frat party last weekend," JoJo said. She swallowed hard. "Let's just leave it at that."

"Were you assaulted?" Makayla asked, eyes burning with anger.

"No. Nothing like that."

"Tell me what happened!"

JoJo took a deep breath. Closed her eyes. Shook her

head. She should never have let the first word slip. It was just too humiliating. Even more humiliating than 104-23.

Makayla leaned close, digging an elbow into JoJo's side.

"It's really nothing," JoJo said. "It's making a mountain out of a molehill."

"Tell me!"

"I should have known better."

"It isn't your fault!" Makayla said in a fierce whisper.

JoJo swallowed hard, the lump in her throat making it take what felt like minutes.

"Tell me!"

"Okay," JoJo said, knowing from experience she couldn't hold off Makayla indefinitely. With something like this, she was like a pit bull. "The boy was *so* out of my league. I should have suspected something. I know I'm ugly—"

"You're not ugly!"

"I know what I am, and I sure ain't pretty. So when this guy from one of my classes—he looks like Brad Freaking Pitt and has never said a word to me before—when he asked me to be his date for the party, I should have known better. But I'm a fool. Hope is a terrible thing. I hoped he might be different. Just like we had hopes we could play with those teams this weekend."

JoJo took in another deep breath and exhaled slowly, trying to make sure she didn't make an even bigger fool of herself by breaking into tears.

"Well, turns out it wasn't a regular party," she finally said. "It was a Pig Party. The boys had each kicked in twenty dollars, and whoever had invited the ugliest girl would win."

"*Oh!*" Makayla said, sounding like she'd been punched in the gut. "Oh my God."

"I don't know if my date won. I hope not. Actually, better me than someone else. But it doesn't really matter. You don't have to be the queen of that particular ball. Just getting the invite is enough."

"That is so wrong!"

"So this weekend was just really bad timing. Getting robbed of my dignity on the basketball court so soon after getting robbed of it off the court was just—"

JoJo couldn't continue. She bowed her head and tried to hold back the tears. If they broke through, they'd come in torrents and she'd soon break into wracking sobs.

"You are an attractive woman!" Makayla said.

"Stop it!" JoJo said, her throat tight.

"You aren't like me or like swimsuit models. You're big and beautiful! Statuesque!"

JoJo shook her head. She didn't believe it for a second.

Makayla moved her mouth to JoJo's ear, and whispered. "If I weren't in a relationship and you were into girls, I'd do you right now!"

The words stopped JoJo's runaway emotions dead in their tracks. A snicker escaped from her lips.

"Right now, sister! I'd do you right now," Makayla cooed, in a clearly teasing tone. She moaned softly. "You'd be liking girls before you could say, 'I hate sausage!'"

JoJo giggled. Then giggled some more when Makayla puffed warm air into her ear. And broke into laughter when Makayla began to lick her ear lobe.

"Okay!" JoJo said. "You made your point. Whatever it was."

"If you ever even think the word 'ugly' again, I'll have to do to your lips what I just did to your ears," Makayla said with a salacious grin. "And then I'll have to go to other parts of your beautiful, *statuesque* body. Got that?"

"Got it! Whew!" JoJo said, smiling and waving the air in mock ardor. "Why can't you be a man?"

"Why can't you play for my team?" Makayla winked.

"I wish I did," JoJo said. "I tried out one time, but I got cut."

They both chuckled, but it was true. JoJo had experimented one time out of part curiosity and part frustration with the male species, which sometimes seemed to be the lowest of all lifeforms. But that wasn't how she was wired.

"Just find another me with a dick," Makayla said.

"Yeah, but that'll mean he *is* a dick."

"You'll find one that isn't," Makayla said. "I don't have personal experience, but I've heard they aren't totally extinct."

JoJo smiled. "Thanks, Makayla. You're something else."

"You sure you okay?"

JoJo nodded, and patted her heart.

IF ANY OF THE BROTHERS BACK HOME EVER FOUND out about this, Derek Peters figured he'd have to shoot himself. Bad enough to get cut from the team. This was worse, at least in their eyes. Much worse.

He was sitting in the office of the women's, not the men's, basketball coach. The air smelled of perfume, or at least he imagined it did. He supposed it was possible that it was all in his head and was just air freshener, but it still smelled too feminine for him. A coach's office should smell like a locker room. It should come right to the edge of *stink*, and if it toppled over into the odor pit, that was fine, too. Derek had come to love that foul, sweaty smell over the years, and had feared the day it would fill his nostrils no more.

He'd thought that day had already come. But here his scrawny, toothpick-thin ass was, wearing his practice jersey, white with the blue falcon on the chest, his head shaved, heart pounding.

Still fighting.

The tight ten-by-twelve room held the coach's wooden desk with papers stacked in neat piles on its perimeter, her chair, the folding metal chair he was sitting in, a John Wooden "Pyramid of Success" poster on his right, and an oversized whiteboard on the wall to his left. The whiteboard was filled with slogans printed in big, black, block letters. Good ones he'd seen before over the years. "Get 1% Better Every Day." "Champions are Made in Practice." And a personal favorite he'd found difficult to cling to at times like this, "Winners and Losers in Life are Self-determined. Only the Winners are Willing to Admit It."

Behind her desk sat Coach Suzie Hyatt, an African American woman of about forty with broad shoulders, a short Afro, and the attitude of an old-school nun.

"You're not here for you, you're here for them," she said, pointing her index finger toward the basketball court where the rhythmic dribbling of balls had just begun. "If you're going to have a bad attitude and think this is beneath you, then get out now."

In truth, it was hard for Derek not to have a bad attitude. Hard not to have a *horrendous* attitude, and think this was so beneath him it was humiliating. But he needed his scholarship.

A junior at Fairview, he'd worked hard his first two years both in the classroom and on the basketball court. He wasn't going to be awarded a Rhodes scholarship, and he wasn't headed for the NBA, but he'd done his best.

Never in danger of academic ineligibility or even probation but no threat for the Dean's List, Derek was still proud of his results in the classroom. Many people had no appreciation for how hard it had been to transition from a godawful inner city high school to a university like Fairview, then study in a real major like Business, not the glorified basket weaving courses some teammates took to stay eligible. His hoop scholarship had never been a tool to get him into the NBA. At five feet eleven inches, you had to practically be the next Michael Jordan in athleticism to have a pro ball future, especially if you were Black. Derek could dunk, but he was no Michael. Pro ball wasn't in his future. His scholarship was to get him a real career and a good life after his four years.

On the court, he'd been slowed by knee problems. As soon as he got in a groove, the knee would sideline him. Up and down, up and down, both years. He'd given it his best and had hoped for a breakthrough junior year, but he'd never gotten the chance.

The new men's coach, a white snake-charmer by the name of Luke Kaufman, had decided to partially clean house and go with his own recruits. He'd cut Derek and two other juniors on at least half scholarships—perhaps not coincidentally all African Americans—and been pleased to see the other two transfer to other schools. Off the books. To Derek, he said with an almost sadistic joy that the only way to retain the scholarship would be to serve as a practice player.

On the women's team.

And if Derek didn't like it, he could pay his own tuition or transfer to some school who'd give an athletic scholarship to a player who'd achieved pretty much nothing in his two years.

Neither possibility had even an icicle's chance in Hell.

Derek had only lasted on the men's team through early December because of delays in getting academic eligibility for new recruits being added for the second semester. Which had led him now to Coach Suzie Hyatt's office and her take it or leave it offer. With his balls in a vise, Derek smiled so she wouldn't turn the crank.

"I'll do whatever I can to help," he said.

"Good," Coach Hyatt said. "Get out there and be prepared to do whatever I ask. We're in the small gym today. Remember, whatever it takes. It's about them, not you."

Out on the court where the team was warming up with layup drills, his eyes were instantly drawn to the two captains, identified by a blue C stitched into their jerseys above the right breast. They were as different as could be. One was a petite sister with cornrows in the front of her black hair and box braids in back down to her shoulders. A classic beauty who could adorn any magazine cover. Tiny and chatting up a storm.

The other was a big white girl even taller than he was with the beefy, strong build of a powerlifter. His kind of woman, whether white or Black. He was instantly attracted.

But that wasn't what he was here for. *Don't screw this up*, he reminded himself as the bouncing balls and calls of encouragement echoed in the small gymnasium with its ten rows of wooden stands, and sneakers squeaked on the floor. This might be a crushing blow to his pride—forget *might be*, it unquestionably *was* a crushing blow—but he needed that scholarship.

Pay the price. Eyes on the prize. He had a million more where those two came from. He would get through this. He'd hold his head high at graduation. Whatever it took.

On his third time through the layup line, he did what he always did his third time through the line. He dunked. Didn't even think about it. It was part of his ritual as long as his knee was healthy.

Behind him, Derek heard the steely words: "overcompensating A-hole." A split second later, a ferocious elbow drove into the middle of his ribs. He dropped to one knee.

It had been the attractive big white woman.

THE LAST THING JoJo NEEDED IN THE FIRST practice after the Mistletoe Madness humiliation was to have one of the swinging dicks from the men's team show up. Makayla had made her feel better, a lot better. If Makayla's spirit could be bottled, chronic depression would be cured.

But the wounds from the tournament—*104-23!*—still stung. And though it had been a Mass State third-stringer, a woman, who had launched that final, rub-your-nose-in-it three-pointer, JoJo saw a man in her mind's eye: the male Mass State coach, the ultimate Mass-hole famous for running up the score. And if not him, then that cruel frat boy who had asked her to be his guest at the Pig Party.

And though this new guy at practice—a really good-looking, thin African American with a shaved head—looked nothing like the fiftyish white, ugly, Masshole coach with black-rimmed glasses, or the handsome-in-a-different-way, white frat boy, the humiliated part of JoJo's brain still made the transference.

The new guy was a just another dick. It was baked into the male chromosomes.

He'd proved the point less than five minutes into the practice. Coach Hyatt had introduced him as the latest practice player from the men's team. The women's team had had several in JoJo's three years, and they served an important function, especially for a center like her. At six-two and built like a bull, she was taller and stronger than everyone else on the team. A matchup nightmare. She could score down low at will and outmuscle everyone else for rebounds.

So she got no better during scrimmages. They almost encouraged bad habits. Then when she went up against opponents as big and as strong as she was, they destroyed her. Like had happened in what she had come to think of as the Mistletoe Massacre.

Humiliated her.

So a guy who could be as tall as she was without being freakishly tall, and as strong because of the mere presence of muscle-building testosterone coursing through his system, could challenge her to become a better player.

Which was a good thing even if most of them just played out the semester, unable to take what one of them had confided was merciless ribbing from the guys pretending to be their friends. Tutus and ballerina slippers left on their beds. A package of lacy panties. Gay porn. As if it hadn't been tough enough for these players to get cut from the men's team, ending their hopes and dreams.

More evidence for JoJo that there was an A-hole component in the male chromosomes.

So she'd treated the previous male practice players with a dignity that their alleged friends couldn't find if given a damned compass. And used them to get better.

But this guy had arrived at the wrong time. Right after the Mistletoe Massacre *and* the Pig Party. The worst of timing. Plus, he wasn't even six feet tall. Maybe a hundred sixty pounds soaking wet. A guy shorter and lighter than she was would be of limited usefulness, at least for her. Maybe a help to the others, but the wrong guy at the wrong time.

No matter how good looking he was. That didn't matter on the team. And the frat boy had been good looking, too. How had that worked out?

Then not even five minutes into his first practice with the team, the new guy dunked.

Dunked! Hey, look at me! I've got testosterone and you don't! I can pee standing up and you can't! The men's team has thousands of fans and you don't! I got cut from the men's team, but I still can humiliate you!

A dick!

JoJo was delighted that she was perfectly positioned to respond, beneath the basket to take his layup-turned-dunk and feed it to the next player in line.

"Overcompensating A-hole!" she muttered in a near-holler, and then whirled, elbows flying, to deliver the appropriate exclamation point to the swinging dick's ribs.

It was the most satisfying thing she'd done in a long time.

It bordered on orgasmic.

DEREK NEVER SAW THE "WELCOME-TO-OUR-TEAM" elbow coming. It dropped him to his knees, gasping.

"What the hell was that for?" he asked reflexively, realizing after the fact that the accompanying "overcompensating A-hole" comment provided all the explanation he really needed.

He looked at the woman they called JoJo, the one who'd delivered the blow. Damn, that was a lot of woman! A strong woman! Damn, he found her attractive, but she'd made abundantly clear the feeling was not mutual.

The venom kept spewing.

"We lost a game this weekend by eighty points!" she yelled, her face turning blood red. "Eighty points! Including a three-pointer in the final minute! We don't need a testosterone-spewing, flaming A-hole to make us feel any worse!"

Derek, still down on one knee, winced. "I didn't mean anything by it."

"Didn't mean anything! Just figured you'd put us in our place and show off that you can do something none of us can. Break the no-dunking rule before any one of us even knows your name."

Derek climbed to his feet.

"My name is Derek. Derek Peters. And this is the first I've heard of a no-dunking rule."

He thought of putting his hand out for a conciliatory handshake, but wondered if this... this amazon... would rip it off and feed it to the rest of the team, now all gathered around.

"Coach didn't tell you?" she asked, fire in her eyes.

"No!"

"Well she shouldn't have had to! Only a handful of women in college can do it. It doesn't even happen much in the WNBA. Why else would you do it if not to make us feel small?"

Derek's heart sank. It was obvious to him now. He'd felt the sour taste of humiliation many times in his life for any number of reasons. Because he was Black. Dirt poor. And perceived as inferior either blatantly or subtlety, each time cutting deeply into his heart. It pained him to have been on the delivering end this time.

"I... I didn't even think about it. It's just a habit."

"Break it!"

Coach Hyatt rushed over. "JoJo, what's the problem?"

JoJo's jaw set and her nostrils flared. "Michael Jordan here decided to dunk." Derek blinked, but said nothing, as JoJo kept going. "Just what we needed after last weekend. A swinging dick who's overcompensating."

Derek spread his hands wide, wondering if his scholarship was hanging in the balance or already gone. He was afraid of the answer. If he had to grovel, he'd grovel. Dignified or not.

"I didn't know," he said. "I'm sorry. I should have realized. It'll never happen again. No dunking or anything like it. You'll be glad I'm here. I'll fit in. I promise."

"Make sure you do," Coach Hyatt said with a stern glare. She blew her whistle. "Okay, everyone. Listen up."

By the end of the practice, Derek was as soaked in sweat as in the old days on the men's team. The challenges were different, but he'd still had to work at it. He'd noticed the woman—JoJo—eying him a few times, apparently sizing him up. And he was sure he'd eyed her a few times himself. Not in any distracted way. The focus had always been on basketball. But during breaks, he'd been unable to help himself.

As the rest of the team filed into the women's locker room, Derek sidled up to JoJo.

"Got a sec?" he asked. "I made a really bad first impression. I'm not like that."

"Sorry about that elbow," she said wistfully. "Guess I overdid it."

He shrugged. "I deserved it."

"Maybe a bit, but I didn't mean to drop you to your knees."

"How often do you sharpen those elbows?" he asked with mock grin, rubbing his ribs.

"Before every new swinging dick joins the team," she said.

"Mission accomplished," Derek said, liking this woman a lot. "Hey, could we get a cup of coffee?" When she seemed to hesitate ever so slightly, he added, "Finish clearing the air?"

~

JoJo had hesitated only because the Pig Party scars were still so fresh on her soul. She couldn't imagine what this gorgeous man could see in her. If he, too, was going to ridicule her or rob her of whatever slivers of dignity she still clung to, she wouldn't be able to stand it. But she thought she'd seen something in his eyes at practice, something in the way he looked at her.

So she'd decide to gamble on a man one last time.

She knew this would never be called a date, but Derek had asked to meet her and her alone. Not her and Makayla, the other team captain and the one who was gorgeous and African American and everything that men wanted. Who would never in a million years be invited to a Pig Party. Admittedly, she was also gay, but Derek didn't necessarily know that.

Then again, Makayla hadn't all but decked him with a flying elbow. On purpose. JoJo held that honor all for herself. And Derek had asked to have coffee with *her*. She could only shake her head.

They slid into a booth with a red-and-green checkered tablecloth that read "Season's Greetings" in gold cursive. Against the wall was a black napkin-holder with a six-inch Christmas tree on top of it. A rectangular dish with a menorah painted on the side was filled with packets of sugar and sugar-substitutes, and a circular hole at one end with wooden stirrers sticking up. The smell of coffee and heated milk for lattes filled the air. Conversation and clicking laptop keyboards echoed from the other nineteen booths arrayed in an L-shape.

"I feel really badly about making such a bad first impression," Derek said. "Both to the team and you individually."

Her individually? What did that mean? JoJo didn't want to read too much into it. This was, after all, a very good-looking man and she was... she was what she was. So she played it safe.

"That elbow of mine wasn't exactly the greatest introduction either," she said with a weak grin.

"I swear to you that dunking on my third layup really is my ritual. No lie. But—" He shrugged. "It still stings getting cut from the men's team. I might have been overcompensating. Just not in the way you were insinuating." He grinned. "I might have subconsciously been trying to impress you, too. Without realizing it."

JoJo blew the steam off her coffee. Cautiously, she asked, "Impress me or the whole team?"

"Yeah, the whole team, but you especially."

The words took her breath away. Her especially? Did they really mean what she thought they meant? How could that be true? Or was he just another cruel A-hole, setting her up so he could laugh when he knocked her down?

Feeling timid as a mouse, the exact opposite of the woman who'd delivered a haymaker of an elbow to this man just hours ago, JoJo asked in barely more than a whisper, "Why me?"

Derek, who'd been leaning forward as if hanging on her

every word, sank back into the booth. He rocked there for a moment, took a breath, then leaned forward again.

"If this is inappropriate and I'm making you feel at all uncomfortable, just say so and I'll stop. You won't have to say so twice. But... I'm attracted to you. Some guys like the Anorexia Annies out there, but not me. You're a lot of woman and I like that." He grinned wryly. "And you've got just a wee bit of spirit in you, too."

JoJo wasn't sure whether to shout for joy or to cry. She was afraid to be happy. So she blurted out the words that her heart couldn't hold back.

"Are you making fun of me?"

Derek recoiled. "No! Hell, no! Why would I do that? Why would anyone do that?"

He was either telling the truth or he was the greatest actor in the world. *Why would anyone do that?* That was a question JoJo had asked so many times with no answer.

"There are some cruel guys out there," JoJo said. "God help you if that's all you're doing."

Derek put his forearms on the table. "I swear I'm telling the truth. I'd never hurt you. With someone else, I might crack a joke that I'd never hurt someone with sharper elbows than mine"—he flashed a smile—"but I'm not joking."

JoJo could muster only one word. "Wow."

"We've got a lot in common really," Derek said.

JoJo blinked. "Yeah, I'm a big white woman and you're a good-looking Black man. Lots in common."

"We've both taken it on the chin recently," he said. "Major blows to our pride. It still stings that I got cut. Hurts real bad. I wasn't good enough. I hate that.

"You're hurting over the Mistletoe tournament. And seems like something else. We're both hurting."

JoJo stiffened. "I don't want your pity."

"Pity ain't what I'm offering. Not at all. And I don't want yours. This ain't no pity party. You're a beautiful woman. No reason to pity you at all. I only see reasons to fall in love with you."

JoJo gasped.

"I'm sorry," Derek said quickly, holding out a hand as if to steady her. "I went too fast. We haven't even had our first official date—unless that's what this is—and here I'm talking about falling in love. But—"

"Keep talking," JoJo said, her voice cracking.

"What?"

"Keep talking about falling in love. The faster the better."

Derek smiled warmly. He put his hand out. JoJo wrapped her hand around his and squeezed.

"This might be too fast," Derek said, "but there's some mistletoe by the entrance that we could check out when we leave."

JoJo nodded. She took the tiniest sip of her coffee, then set it down. "The coffee here really is terrible."

Derek took a similar lightning-fast sip. "Awful."

"Wretched."

"Undrinkable."

They paid the bill for the dreadful coffee, and left in a hurry. The mistletoe, however, was outstanding.

And they'd be back.

The Run of Her Life

Introduction to The Run of Her Life

IF STORIES THAT INCLUDE A *TWILIGHT ZONE* TYPE of impossible twist on the real world aren't your thing, humor me. Please. I think it'll be worth your while.

Let me explain.

"The Run of Her Life" is one of two stories I've written set in Cave Creek, a mythical old mining town north of Las Vegas where impossible things happen. (My other Cave Creek story, "Stepping Into the Light" is not a romance, so it's included in *The Soulmate Junkie and Other Stories of Fantasy and Science Fiction*. That collection is scheduled to release one month after this one.) Dean Wesley Smith created this fictional town and has so far released four books in the series: his novel *Card Sharp Silver*, and three related anthologies, *Bitter Mountain Moonlight* (Past), *Open Ended Threat* (Present), and *Promise in the Gold* (Future).

"The Run of Her Life," which appeared in *Open Ended Threat*, is firmly grounded in present day reality. That is, until... it isn't. But it's a romance through and through. A

really fun one to write and, I hope, a really fun one for you
to read.

The Run of Her Life

LISA TOWNSEND WAS PLASTERED IN SWEAT AND loved it. It stung her eyes, tasted salty on her lips, and drenched her matching neon green running shorts and sports-bra top. Only her neon green running shoes remained dry. She never felt more alive than in the middle of a long run, especially on a pebble-strewn, uphill, dirt trail like this one not even wide enough for a car. Pockets of scrub trees and brush dotted the desert landscape on both sides. Craggy mountains rose in the distance straight ahead.

This was life.

She glanced at her running watch and saw her GPS-calculated pace for the last mile. Under eight minutes a mile, about what she'd averaged running the Boston Marathon last year. And this pace was even better because of having to loop back for Paul, her boyfriend who'd damned well better become her husband soon. He was much slower than she was, his gait totally unlike her gazelle-like springing-forward motion and more like an elephant clomping along even though he was quite fit. But kudos to him for joining her.

Then again, that had been their deal. One week in Cave Creek just north of Las Vegas where she could indulge her joy of morning runs and her fascination with old ghost towns, which were plentiful in the area. They'd spend the next week in Vegas itself where he'd play poker, she'd play blackjack, and they'd go to shows and enjoy the nightlife.

"If I don't want to strangle you after the first week," Paul had said, "and if you don't want to strangle me after the second, then maybe we're meant for each other after all."

He'd thought that was a whole lot funnier than she did. Lisa had smiled, but his pervasive use of "maybe" and "if" and every other possible waffling term was wearing thin. So as far as she was concerned, this would be the vacation in which they decided for once and for all if they'd spend their lives together. She wanted an answer and dammit, she wanted it now.

She was twenty-seven and while that was hardly old these days even for someone like herself who wanted to have kids, she felt the ominous Big Three Oh-Shit looming on the horizon. She didn't want to be like so many of her friends, strung along aimlessly year after year with no true commitment until finally they got dropped off in Dump City and had to start all over again. That wasn't going to be her.

What the hell was Paul's problem?

Everyone considered her attractive. Long, dirty blonde hair. Hazel brown eyes. A pretty face, albeit with a bit of a pug nose. Exceptionally fit to the point of being the envy of her friends. She checked all the superficial boxes plus she was fun to be with, a good person, and based on Paul's every reaction, a really good lover.

So what the hell was his problem? Shit or get off the pot!

They'd met online and felt an instant attraction for each other. He was six feet tall, well-built with sandy hair, a nice smile, a kind disposition, and a good sense of humor. He worked in the financial services industry, she in industrial real estate, both in the suburbs of Boston. Over a year ago, they'd moved in together. They weren't a *perfect* fit for each other, but who was? This was real life, not Hollywood. Sometimes you had to take the two pieces of the puzzle that didn't *quite* line up—an overlap here and a gap there—and just jam them together, rough edges and all, until they did fit.

Take "close but no cigar" and make a damned cigar out of it.

At least that's what Lisa thought. But she wasn't going to drag Paul to the alter. Marriage wasn't going to be like this run, where she went racing ahead and then had to keep looping back every half mile or so and let him catch up. He was either going to stick with her all the way—and with enthusiasm—or not.

As he said at the poker table all the time, fold or go all in.

A bit after a rise and a bend in the trail, she was about to circle back when she spotted a rock outcropping ahead on the right, twenty-feet high at its peak and thirty-five feet wide. She paused her watch—she had no intention of letting a pee break tarnish her hard-earned pace—and scampered over to the back side of the rocky knoll. She was about to slide her neon shorts and underwear down when the air about her began to buzz and sparkle.

She stopped. Looked more closely.

Ten feet ahead of her was a curious shimmering, arch-like shape barely her height. She stepped closer and tried to peek through to the other side.

What was she seeing?

Was that an old mining town barely discernable in the distance? A ghost town visible from this hillside vantage point that hadn't been on the tourist maps? But that was impossible! She knew where all the ghost towns were.

And that direction was no ghost town. It was Cave Creek!

"Paul?" she called out over her shoulder, but got no reply. He hadn't caught up yet. Perfect!

She stepped closer to the arch... closer still...

Then *through* it.

She couldn't make out any details from this distance, but Lisa instinctively recognized the town as old, as definitively categorized as a black-and-white movie. An old-time mining town. But how could that be?

She felt an overwhelming urge to race down there this instant, without a second delay. Without turning her head away from the mysterious sight, she called out, "Paul?" and for the first time felt annoyance that he could barely manage a ten-mile-an-hour pace. It would take *forever* to get down there.

And where the hell was he? Get the lead out, darling!

She turned to go back and get him, but—

The arch-like shape was gone!

And the rock outcropping was different. Rougher and more jagged. Taller. Not the same at all.

Lisa sprinted around it. Back to the trail.

Or rather... where the trail had been.

There was no trail now. None in sight. Just an endless stretch of desert sand, scrub trees and brush, and the occasional rocky hillside or Joshua tree, its gnarled and twisting limbs reaching to the sky.

"Paul!" Lisa yelled. *"Paul!"*

No trail. And no Paul.

IF TODAY DIDN'T PROVE HIS LOVE FOR LISA, PAUL Schofield wasn't sure what would. (Other than a marriage proposal, of course, the perpetual fly in their ointment.) But didn't he deserve some credit? Just a stone's throw from Vegas, and what were they doing first thing in the morning?

Running!

Not playing poker or blackjack or sampling succulent delicacies at a breakfast buffet.

Running! *In... the... desert!*

That wasn't love? That wasn't enough?

His idea of getting hot and sweaty didn't involve running shoes and shorts at all. It involved removing them.

And everything else. Getting hot and sweaty the old-fashioned way. *That's* what they should be doing right now!

He'd be a whole lot more motivated to run, he mused as the sweat stung his eyes and his bright orange T-shirt and shorts clung to his skin, if Lisa stayed perpetually fifteen feet ahead of him instead of racing off so she was nowhere in sight. Seeing her put an extra spring in his step. He absolutely adored the view of her lithe figure moving along, her dirty blonde hair tied back in a ponytail that bounced on her shoulders, the tanned skin of her midriff and legs sleek with sweat, and that cute little butt swaying back and forth.

He *loved* that view. He'd run every day if it could be like that.

He supposed that would be creepy coming from someone else. Lisa spoke often of the leers and catcalls sent her way when running alone. There was a reason she carried a cigarette-lighter-sized container of pepper spray in a pocket of her shorts. There were just too many predators out there.

But the two of them had been living together for over a year now. Wasn't it a *good* sign that they hadn't fallen into a comfortable rut of near boredom with each other? Wasn't it a *damned* good sign that looking at her wiggling backside still evoked his desire?

He had to admit, though, it was also another piece of evidence that Lisa was right, it was time to ask for her hand in marriage. The other evidence was even more compelling, most notably that they unquestionably loved each other and were compatible—this miserable, godforsaken run being the exception that proved that rule. Paul just had to remove his last niggling doubts, almost certainly fueled by his parent's bitter divorce, or risk missing out on potentially the best thing that could ever happen to him.

But he needed to be sure.

Paul rounded a turn in the pebble-strewn trail and looked ahead at a straightaway that moved steadily uphill.

Lisa wasn't on it.

A sliver of fear sliced through him. She should at least be a speck in the distance. There were no visible dips or turns in the trail to hide her. She was fast and he was slow, but there was no way she shouldn't still be visible. In fact, Lisa often liked to choose extended uphill stretches like this as a workout within a workout, something she'd specifically loop back to do multiple times.

But she was nowhere to be seen.

He looked all around. Nothing but desert sand, scrub trees and brush. That, and a wide, twenty-foot-high rock outcropping off to the right. Could she have gone around it to relieve herself, and... and something...

A sick feeling rumbled in his gut. A sour taste formed in the back of his mouth.

He raced around the rocky knoll, sprinting like he'd never sprinted before, turning the corner and—

Nothing!

"Lisa!" he yelled, not even trying to hide the panic in his voice. *"Lisa!"*

Nothing.

With trembling hands, Paul pulled his phone out of his pocket and removed it from its protective zip-lock bag. Relieved that even out here it got a signal, he speed-dialed Lisa. She didn't carry a phone, considering it too bulky, but had cellular service on her watch.

The call went straight to voicemail.

"*I can't answer right now,*" she said cheerfully on the recording, slicing a dagger into Paul's heart. "*Leave a message and I'll get back to you.*"

Paul had all he could do to keep from falling apart.

"Call me!" he shouted into the phone. "Where are you? Call me!"

He called five more times, each one going straight to her voicemail and a voice he suddenly feared he'd never hear again. His heart pounded more fiercely than on any of his runs with Lisa.

Hands shaking uncontrollably, he punched in the digits for 911.

~

LISA CALLED FOR PAUL AGAIN AND AGAIN, mystified at where the trail had gone and how the landscape had changed. Terrified at what had happened to Paul.

She glanced at her watch, about to push the side button and call him. But the watch, which had moments before shown her 7:53 per mile pace was now flashing *Searching... Searching... Searching.*

Lisa knew it wasn't searching for a cellular tower or a Wi-Fi connection. It was searching for a GPS satellite. And finding none. And if it couldn't find a satellite...

She tried calling Paul anyway.

No signal.

She was alone. Totally alone.

What the hell was she supposed to do now? She'd follow the running trail back to Cave Creek, but—

There wasn't any trail!

How could she ever find her way back? The trail had twisted and turned and dipped and risen so many times, she wasn't sure which way to go, not through the desert with all its scrub trees and brush that all looked alike. Even the distinctive rock outcropping beside her didn't look like she had remembered it. And there was a Joshua tree here, its limbs sparse and twisted, that she swore hadn't been there minutes earlier.

Based on the position of the sun, still rising in the East, she could guess as to the direction of Cave Creek, but that couldn't be right because that was the same general direction as the ghost town off in the distance.

Bewildered and confused, Lisa fought back her rising sense of panic—*what the hell had happened. Where was she? Where the hell was Paul? What the holy hell was going on?*— and trotted back to the other side of the rocky knoll.

The vast panorama of the desert was broken only by the ghost town off in the distance. Or what she had assumed was a ghost town based on how old the buildings looked from afar.

Could she find help there? Or at least get answers to what the hell had happened? The only alternative was to sit here and do nothing.

Lisa couldn't do that.

She looked again at her watch. *Searching... Searching... Searching.* Tried calling Paul on it once again. *No signal.*

Nothing. She was totally alone.

She hollered one more time for Paul, knowing it was pointless, then scribbled a note for him in the sand near where the trail had been. If he was here somewhere, if he was still alive—her heart broke at having to even consider the alternative—he'd know where to find her.

With one final look back, she was off.

PAUL PUNCHED THE DIGITS FOR 911 AGAIN, practically fracturing both his index finger and the phone's screen at the same time.

Almost twenty minutes and nothing! Where the hell were they?

They had called back to verify his location, but apparently *they hadn't verified shit!*

Where were they?

He knew it was remote up here with much of the trail inaccessible by car, but the love of his life was missing, goddammit, and he could just see that somewhere her blood-splattered body lay motionless, perhaps lifeless, and *nobody was doing anything!*

He had run up and down the trail, backward and forward from where this rock outcropping dominated the landscape. He'd run far further than she could possibly be, calling her name at the top of his voice—*"Lisa! Lisa! Lisa!"* —calling over and over until his throat was raw and sore and he could barely manage a croak.

"Lisaaaaaaaaa!"

Nothing!

The haunting silence tore him apart.

So when the 911 operator assured him this second time that help was indeed on the way, Paul almost bit her head off.

"If it's on the way, then where the hell is it? I called twenty fucking minutes ago!"

Paul heard the sound of an engine first. Then an all-terrain police vehicle looking much like a jeep painted in cop-car black-and-white colors crested the hill, straddling the trail, and stopped at his side. A single officer in plainclothes emerged with a German shepherd.

One officer? Where was a full search-and-rescue team? Six people or a dozen. Why wasn't a helicopter making an aerial search?

One plainclothes officer was the best they could do?

"You Paul Schofield?" the officer asked. He looked ex-Marine, maybe Special Forces. Crew cut. Jaw of granite. Eyes of ice. Khakis. Short-sleeved blue shirt, tight in the chest, bulging in the biceps.

Hard.

As the officer began asking the most basic, maddening questions, the German shepherd sniffed Paul. Wagged its tail. Sniffed the ground.

More questions.

The German shepherd sniffed Paul again, then the ground. It headed around the rock outcropping to the other side. Began to bark furiously.

The officer, with Paul in his wake, raced to the dog's side. It barked, then growled, barked, then growled, hackles raised, glued to one spot.

It wouldn't move.

"What's it doing?" Paul asked in a voice both hopeful and fearful.

The officer didn't answer. He looked at his watch, then walked in a widening circle around the dog.

"*Answer me!*" Paul demanded. "*What's the dog doing? And what the hell are you doing?*"

The rock-hard officer looked at his watch one more maddening time, then locked eyes with Paul.

"I know where she is."

LISA'S PACE SLOWED AND ALMOST STOPPED AS SHE grew closer to the ghost town, sweat streaming down her face, mystified anew at what she was seeing.

It wasn't a ghost town.

There were people there, living people, only a few here and there on the outskirts, but a bustling crowd of several hundred on and around a Main Street that extended for at least a mile, maybe more. They were dressed like actors on a giant movie set depicting a Western town from a time a hundred years ago, the men wearing wide-brimmed hats and the women plain, ankle-length dresses. Or perhaps they were a host of groups performing a historical reenactment. Or this was some life-like historical play put on for tourists wanting to see life in a mining town in the early 1900s. But none of that made sense.

This was *too* authentic. It wasn't a movie set or a reenactment of a staged play.

It was *real.* Impossible, but real.

Lisa couldn't believe her eyes. She hid behind a rickety, old wooden shack just beyond the outskirts of the town, peeking to see what on any other day would be a history buff's dream come true.

Most of the people were men but there were a few

women. And horses, horse-drawn wagons, mules, men pushing wheelbarrows, and a stagecoach. A crack of a whip sounded amidst the cacophony of shouting voices, horses whinnying, wagons creaking, and a far-off whistle blowing.

But what had struck Lisa first was the overpowering, nauseating stench. Hitting her long before she got near enough to make out any people, it made her eyes water. The place smelled of rotten eggs, horse manure, a row of ten ramshackle shacks this side of the main street that unquestionably had to be outhouses.

How could these people stand it? The stench, more than anything, proved conclusively that this was no tourist trap Lisa had missed in her planning. You didn't lay out something this grand and authentic, then leave the tourists gagging at the vile odor and gasping for clean air.

Somehow, these people could not only bear it, but ignore it, too. Lisa couldn't understand how, but she didn't see anyone bending over and retching like she'd felt on the verge of doing since getting downwind of the town. The townspeople went about their business as if they had no sense of smell at all.

Both men and women. They walked hurriedly along Main Street from one business to another. At this near end of Main Street stood the most impressive building of all, the two-story Golden Dream Hotel. It had a high-pitched roof and a front porch beneath which a dozen people sat in the shade. From there, those the buildings quickly became shabby: a general store, apothecary, blacksmith, horse barn, seven or eight saloons, gambling dens, a bakery and restaurant, cobbler, dentist, newspaper office, trading post, and telegraph office.

Then Lisa saw two buildings that made her jaw drop. The post office and town hall. But not just any nameless post office and town hall.

The Cave Creek Post Office. The Cave Creek Town Hall.

This was Cave Creek? But how?

WHEN THE OFFICER TOLD PAUL HE KNEW WHERE Lisa was, Paul's head all but exploded.

"*Where? Is she okay?*"

"I believe she's safe," the officer said. "But it's not so much a matter of *where* she is as *when*."

"*What?*" Paul wasn't in the mood for riddles or nonsense. He just wanted to see Lisa and be sure she was okay.

"Cave Creek is a strange place," the officer said, and Paul belatedly noticed the man wore no identification badge. "That's why I'm here. Las Vegas Metro Police Department handles all of Clark County. I grab the strange cases in and around Cave Creek."

"What the hell is strange about my girlfriend suddenly going missing?" Paul said, trying his best to keep his cool but failing. "Strange is about the *last* fucking word I'd use for it. And if you don't show me where she is, I'm going to fucking explode. Even if you *can* break me in two pieces with your fingers."

The officer maintained his stone face. "I'll need your absolute guarantee that what I say here remains confidential, shared only with your girlfriend."

"Confidential?" Paul was incredulous and beyond impatient. He wanted to scream. "What are you going to say?"

"I can enforce your silence either through physical means or hypnosis, but I must insist—"

"*I'll keep quiet! I'll keep quiet!*" Paul said, doubting he would keep his word. "*Now where the hell is she?*"

"Around Cave Creek, there are a number of things we call slips. Others call them portals. They open into another time in the past or the future. A time machine, if you will. Your girlfriend appears to have stumbled into a known slip called, forgive me if this seems flippant, The Quickie."

Now, Paul did explode.

"*You son of a bitch! You're not even a cop! What have you done with her? I don't care if you can tear me from limb to limb. Go ahead! But I swear to God, I'll kill you if you so much as laid a hand on her. That woman means everything to me!*"

The officer, or whatever he was, didn't bat an eye.

"This slip goes back over a hundred years, to 1914, to be exact. It's called The Quickie because it opens by far more frequently than any other, every half-hour at nine minutes and nine seconds after the hour and the half hour by both sides' reckoning. It's only open for nineteen seconds. Nineteen-point-two-seven-six seconds to be precise, again the same on both sides. Hence, The Quickie. Now you can either call me a liar and threaten me, or you can go through it, find your girlfriend, and get her back here safely."

THIS WAS CAVE CREEK?

Despite the growing mid-morning heat, Lisa began to shiver uncontrollably from her vantage point behind the rickety old shack. She was hopelessly exposed and conspicuous in her neon green shorts and sports bra. This had to be a dream. Or more accurately, a nightmare. Either that, or some kind of horrific hallucination. Had someone slipped something into her food or water this morning?

The alternative was too mind boggling and too terrifying to even consider. Because as impossible as it seemed, this was Cave Creek. Turn-of-the-century Cave Creek.

Just not the right century.

And unless it was a dream or hallucination, the wrong century Cave Creek meant that she'd never see Paul again. They'd never have a chance to see how happy they could be spending their lives together. They'd never have children. Her future with Paul would never happen. Because she was stuck here a century in the past.

Her heart broke at the thought. Even worse, it wasn't just a thought. Her heart broke at *the knowledge.* Because there was no denying what was in plain sight. This was clearly an early 1900s mining town with signs that announced it as Cave Creek, the same town she and Paul had flown almost 3,000 miles to visit for a vacation that would decide once and for all whether they would spend the rest of their lives together.

Well that decision had sure as shit been made, hadn't it! They wouldn't get to spend so much as another single second together!

Paul was gone. Her whole life was gone. Her career, her friends, her family, her happiness. All gone.

Especially Paul.

A broken-hearted sob burst uncontrollably from within her. She put her hand to her mouth, pressed the side of her index finger hard against her lips, and choked back a whimper. She could only imagine what would happen if she were discovered.

But what could she do? When she'd first been able to barely make out people in the distance, the images blurry, she'd begun to sprint toward them, thinking they'd be able to help her. Point her to a police station or a taxi or *something* to get her out of this place. But as she'd drawn closer and seen what couldn't possibly be true, she'd known that no police or taxi or Uber could transport her out of here.

Back to civilization. Back to the twenty-first century. Back to Paul.

No one could help her. And she couldn't help herself. She was stuck here.

But dammit, she had to at least try!

And she would, but how? What could she do? Who would help her?

Knowing she could stand here paralyzed forever, she—in a phrase Paul had used in what felt like a different era—"yanked off the Band-Aid."

Lisa bolted from her cover behind the old shack. Instinctively, she raced toward the Golden Dream Hotel. It looked like by far the town's most refined establishment, if such a thing even existed in a place that smelled like an outhouse. She knew she could not possibly look any more conspicuous in her clothing, or lack thereof, in an era when such things did not exist and such attire would be scandalous even if worn by a prostitute.

Cries of outrage erupted before Lisa made it even a quarter of the way to the hotel. Women gasped and stared, pointing at her as if she were the Devil. One fainted dead away. Men dressed more or less like cowboys gaped, wide-eyed. Shock gave way to disgust or lecherous grins.

"She's just 'bout naked!" one joyously cried.

"She's a Devil!"

"A witch!"

"I'll take her first!" yelled one and howled with laughter.

The crowd began to close in on both sides.

What had she been thinking, Lisa wondered? But what had her choices been? She'd had none.

And she had even fewer choices than none now. She'd never make it to the hotel. The crowd had closed off her path.

And was closing in on her.

She had to get out of here. But where could she go?

Lisa stopped dead in her tracks. Turned and reversed direction.

Feeling a split second of relief that none of the townspeople had closed in behind her—yet!—she sprinted for all she was worth away from them.

She raced for the only destination she could think of. The rock outcropping up the hill where this whole nightmare had started.

But where was it?

She saw mountains in the distance, and a range of rolling hills, but there were craggy clusters of rocks on all of the hills, every one looking the same as the other.

She picked one and ran for her life.

She glanced over her shoulder. A throng of men were hot on her pursuit. She was faster and she could outlast them, she was confident of that, but where could she go? On all sides there was nothing but desert, scrub, the occasional Joshua tree, cluster of rocks, or cacti, then more desert and scrub.

She cursed her impetuosity in coming to this godforsaken town, but what choice had she had? She just have to outrun them all to the hills, find some place to hide, and decide on her next move there. She could outsprint and outlast every one of them. She was sure of it.

Until she heard the hammering sound behind her of galloping hooves.

PAUL FOUGHT BACK HIS RAGE. A PORTAL ACTING as a sort of time machine had transported Lisa a hundred years into the past? What kind of sadistic bastard concocts such total bullshit to taunt someone whose heart is breaking?

The only thing that stopped Paul from trying to tear the guy apart wasn't that he'd surely get torn apart himself. It was the sadist's what-have-you-got-to-lose suggestion that Paul wait a mere two minutes and see if there was something to the insane story,

Other than his dignity if the cop was just making a fool of him, Paul figured what did he have to lose? He had no other options.

So at precisely nine minutes and nine seconds after the hour, with the phony cop and his tethered dog looking on from twenty feet away, Paul Schofield watched the air crackle and sparkle two feet from his face. A shimmering arch-like opening appeared.

Paul's eyes widened and his heart leaped.

Could it be?

"Go!" the cop commanded, digging in his heels and tensing his huge biceps to hold back the suddenly frenzied German shepherd.

Paul stepped through the portal.

Lisa cried out at the sound of galloping hooves behind her. Ahead stretched a mile or so of desert. Dressed in her neon green running garb and shoes, she was sure she could outrun any hostile cowboy in boots. But not even Usain Bolt could outrun a horse. If, that is, Usain Bolt even existed anymore.

She glanced over her shoulder. Three men on horseback rode abreast less than a hundred yards back.

And closing fast.

Plumes of dust billowed in their wake. In her mind, Lisa tasted the gritty particles and choked on their dust. The pounding of the hooves thundered in her ears.

Faster. She had to go faster!

But this was hopeless.

She glanced back again. Fifty yards. Forty.

Then close enough to see a terrifying gleam in one of the men's eyes. His teeth were bared. Smiling.

Lisa shrieked. When that man was done with her—

when the three of them were done with her—she'd wish she were dead. If she weren't dead already.

Choking back a sob, she touched her left shorts pocket. Felt the outline of the lighter-sized pepper spray canister.

Lisa prepared to go down fighting.

PAUL LOOKED AROUND IN DISBELIEF. EVERYTHING had changed. He still stood on a hillside with scrub and sand in every direction, but it was different scrub. Behind him, the outline of the rocks were different, the craggy face more pronounced. There was a Joshua tree.

Even more significantly, the cop and his dog were gone. The cop who had said this would be 1914.

1914!

But of greatest significance by far, there was no sign of Lisa. As if in a trance, he walked around the rock face to where the trail had been, hoping against hope Lisa might be there.

She wasn't. But he saw the message scribbled in the sand along with an arrow pointing down the hillside.

Paul,

Heading to the town for help.

Hope I see you again.

Love you!

Next to the exclamation point, Lisa had drawn the shape of a heart.

Go down fighting, Lisa told herself and slowed to a halt ten feet past a sprawling, gangly Joshua tree. She turned and faced the three rampaging cowboys. They pulled their horses up next to the Joshua tree, dismounted, and tied up their mounts.

Lisa backpedaled slowly. Sweat poured off her. Her heart hammered.

"Please leave me alone," she said, trying unsuccessfully to keep her quivering voice steady.

The men advanced, eying her up and down, leering. They all had the evil gleam in their eyes now.

"I believe we'll get to decide that," the lead cowboy said. He was the tallest of the three, and strode ahead of the other two, one each side, He adjusted the brim of his dust-streaked, black ten-gallon hat. "A devil-woman doesn't get to run around damned near naked, getting boys like us all riled up, and then think she isn't going to do anything about it. Right, boys?"

They echoed their agreement.

Glancing back to be sure she didn't stumble over any clump of vegetation, Lisa kept backpedaling, maneuvering the cowboys further from their horses.

"Leave me alone!" she said, her index finger tensing on the trigger of the pepper spray canister, hidden in her palm.

"Why you walking away from us?" the lead cowboy asked, spreading his hands. "It's not going to change the result. Now come here and get your medicine."

Lisa stepped toward him. The cowboy's eyes widened in surprise. A grin formed on the corners of his mouth.

Holding her breath, Lisa lifted her arm out and sprayed,

going for the eyes. The lead cowboy first. Then the other two.

She turned and sprinted away. Behind her, howls of anguish and outrage erupted.

Lisa ran for her life.

THOUGH HE WAS IMPATIENT TO GET STARTED, Paul first pulled off his bright orange T-shirt, sopping wet as it was, and slid it over a five-foot-high branch on a nearby Joshua tree. As the cop had advised, it would do no good to find Lisa then be unable to find their way back to the portal in a desert where one hill, thicket of brush, and rock face inevitably looked like every other one. Only three branches shot out from the Joshua tree's thin trunk, each of them long, gnarled and twisted, so the sparse branching would let the T-shirt and its orange brilliance act as a beacon guiding them home.

With the maddening delay of that detail over, Paul raced down the gently sloping hillside toward the town. He would find Lisa, no matter what it took. Then he'd never let go. Whether forever stuck in 1914 or back in 2021, he would hold onto her for dear life.

Every few hundred yards, he'd check to see that his bright orange T-shirt was still visible. Occasionally, it would be blocked when he went downhill after cresting a rise, but time after time it reappeared on the next incline.

He still had trouble believing the cop's nonsense even as the vague outlines of old-looking buildings and shacks became visible. Could this really be the Cave Creek of

1914? It seemed preposterous. But he didn't care if it was Cave Creek in 1914, 2014, 2114, or 2214. As long as Lisa was there. And she was safe.

He spotted her after cresting another rise, at first not even recognizing that it was her, just spotting a neon green speck in the distance moving along a background of brown and red dirt. Then it registered.

Lisa!

The purest joy erupted from within him. She was safe! And headed this way. Paul began to sprint toward her. Then stopped.

She was angled in the wrong direction. Not way off, but maybe twenty or thirty degrees, heading for a hillside and rock outcropping that looked right to her, but was wrong. A hillside where there would be no portal to take them back to their own time.

Paul whirled around and looked for the bright orange. Saw it. He was right. Lisa's angle was off.

He sprinted toward her, the neon green speck growing larger, hollering her name with insane joy even though he knew she was too far away to hear it.

"Lisa! Lisa!"

He stopped dead in his tracks. His broad smile fell. Far in the distance, a cloud of dust loomed on the horizon. Was that thundering hoofbeats he heard? Or was it a nightmare of his imagination. Paul tried to calm his pounding heart and leaned closer even while knowing that accomplished nothing.

Yes, those were hoofbeats! And as he watched in horror, the cloud of dust surrounding those animals, whatever they were, was angling toward Lisa! Still a long way away from her, but inching closer.

"Lisa!" Paul called out in sudden panic. "Lisa!"

He jumped up and down, waving his arms.

"Lisa!"

The neon green moved faster, but was still making a beeline in the wrong direction.

Paul jumped up and down, and called her name. He waved his arms.

Nothing.

He suddenly realized his slightly tanned skin blended in too closely with the desert sand. Waving his arms was doing no good. He'd been able to see Lisa only because the neon green was too bold to miss. If only he still had his bright orange T-shirt.

He didn't, but he did have the matching shorts, equally as bright orange. In an instant, he slipped them off, fleetingly thankful he wore underwear beneath them, then began to wave them over his head. The movement of the bright orange might succeed where skin color failed. He knew he looked ridiculous jumping about in his underwear and waving his shorts, but he didn't care.

"Lisa!"

LISA SPOTTED THE LUNATIC WAVING SOMETHING bright orange seconds before she realized it was Paul.

Paul! It was Paul!

It had to be him and his T-shirt! Nothing in this 1900s

world was bright orange like that. She couldn't make out his face, but the orange left no doubt. It was Paul. Even if...

Those were his running shorts, not his T-shirt! And he was waving his shorts while jumping and waving in his underwear.

Lisa would have wept for joy if she hadn't already heard the distant thundering of hooves, and recognized it for what it almost certainly was. More Cave Creek cowboys looking to do her harm. Punish her for her public indecency, and perhaps gain revenge for spraying the other three men with the pepper spray, emptying the canister out on them. She could only imagine what an early 1900s cowboy would ascribe the spray to.

She had known the spray had given her a short-lived reprieve. What little she knew of life in mining towns of this era didn't leave her with any confidence the three cowboys would forgive and forget. If she didn't get back to that magic thing that had somehow dumped her here—and had apparently dumped Paul, too, she hadn't lost him after all!—the town of Cave Creek would tear her from limb to limb.

So she didn't let anything distract her from escaping the galloping mob. Her legs were weak from all the sprinting, but she pushed on.

Faster! Faster!

Suddenly, she realized that Paul was correcting her direction. He was waving his orange shorts and pointing in a direction off to the right from where she was heading. He was pointing to a speck of bright orange in the distance. And now he was sprinting toward it, waving his orange shorts.

She had picked the wrong hillside as her target. The orange was the correct one.

The orange would lead them home. Assuming Paul then had some way of getting them the hell out of here.

Once Paul saw Lisa change course, he knew his one remaining challenge was to get there as soon as, or before, she did. It would do no good if either of them failed to make the next portal opening. She was a lot faster, but had more ground to cover and had to be close to total exhaustion.

He glanced at his watch. Four minutes and change before the next portal opening. Then nineteen seconds to get through it.

If they missed that window—he glanced over his shoulder first at Lisa, then the thundering herd that was closing the gap—if they missed it, they were dead.

Four minutes. It would be close.

Just another fifty yards to go! Lisa recognized the rock outcropping now. And Paul was snagging off a Joshua tree his orange T-shirt that had served as a beacon. Her legs felt like jelly, and her lungs were threatening to explode, but the mob of perhaps fifty riders and their horses were still several hundred yards backs.

"*Faster!*" Paul screamed, dashing over to the outcropping, looking at his watch in sheer desperation. "*We've only got seconds!*"

Lisa didn't understand, but the look in Paul's eyes left no doubt. He knew something that she didn't, and this was life or death. From somewhere deep within, she dug even a little deeper than she thought possible, and on legs of jelly, sprinted even faster.

LISA COLLAPSED IN PAUL'S ARMS AND BEGAN TO weep. But it was too soon for that. The portal still had to appear. It had to open in the next few seconds.

Five... four... three... two... one.

Though her legs wobbled and she felt like dead weight in his arms, Paul held onto Lisa for dear life. And she clung to him.

"Hold on!" he cried.

The air before them crackled and sparkled. As the air around it shimmered, an arch appeared.

With his arms wrapped fiercely around Lisa, hugging her, Paul pulled them both through.

THEY COLLAPSED ON THE GROUND TOGETHER, kissing each other and holding each other tight as the portal closed behind them. They had made it!

Lisa gasped for air, her side heaving, but dove in for another kiss. Neither she nor Paul minded her gasps or the smell of their sweat or the pebbles in the sand that dug into their skin. They gulped air together and started each kiss all over again. After a very long, very sweet time, they finally got to their feet.

Paul, however, dropped back down to one knee.

"I don't need two more weeks to make a decision," he said. "I've never been more sure of anything in my life. I don't have a ring yet, but will you marry me?"

A beatific smile formed on Lisa's mouth.

"Of course! Yes, yes, yes! I will marry you!" Her eyes twinkled. "But two weeks? Didn't that just take you over a hundred years?"

When the Wiener Dogs Come Out to Play

Introduction to *When the Wiener Dogs Come Out to Play*

Almost always for me, a story starts with a character. Not a plot twist or an opening line or even a unique setting. Almost always, the character. If I'm fascinated, or at least mildly interested, I figure the reader will feel the same way. Characters that bore me, however, are almost certain to bore the potential reader.

Sometimes, though, I become more than just fascinated with a character. I fall in love with him or her. Such was the case with Timmy York. Head over heels. Not romantically, of course. But I wanted desperately for Timmy to find happiness.

Does he?

Well, this is a romance so you pretty much know the answer to that question. But I'll ask you a question of my own.

When boy-meets-girl also includes wiener dogs—dachshunds—can it get any better?

When the Wiener Dogs Come Out to Play

Timmy York sold newspapers at the intersection of Truman and White. That was in Key West. In Florida.

He stacked the papers—the *Miami Herald*, the *Florida Keys Free Press*, and the *Key West Citizen*— high in his red wagon at four o'clock in the morning. And Timmy stayed at his corner, wearing his white shorts, white T-shirt, sneakers, and cap until the papers were all sold or it was noon o'clock.

It was almost always hot. And it always smelled of gasoline because of the Chevron station behind him on one side and the Mobil on the other side. And the traffic.

His skin was always deep brown and rough. Almost like leather. And his hair was baked almost blond instead of dark brown. That's because he had been selling papers here seven days a week for a very long time.

As long as he could remember. Maybe since he turned twenty-three. That was almost three years ago. After the bad thing happened in Afghanistan that he couldn't remember anymore. That he didn't want to remember, but couldn't even if he wanted to.

All Timmy knew was that he had the scar on his scalp that always itched and he didn't have his right hand anymore. Just a stump.

No right hand made it harder to give people their newspaper and get their money at the same time. Timmy had to pick up the paper with his left hand, his good hand, then pin it to his chest with his stump. The customer would put the dollar bills in his good hand and Timmy leaned close and they would either pull the newspaper free or he'd shove the money into his pouch and hand them their paper.

Lots of people were nice. A few were mean and laughed at him and called him names that made him feel bad. But mostly, people were friendly and told Timmy to have a good day. Some gave Timmy tips. Like handing him a five or extra ones and telling him to keep the change. On Sundays during the football season, Mr. Leonard from New York even gave Timmy a twenty dollar bill for just two papers as long as he said, "The Patriots suck!"

So Timmy said, "The Patriots suck!" and took the twenty.

For just two papers! Timmy wasn't sure who the Patriots were, but twenty bucks was twenty bucks!

A COUPLE TIMES HE GOT ROBBED, AND THEY BEAT him up pretty bad, but Timmy was tough. A real tough guy for someone with only one fist.

But even tough guys get lonely.

So one day in September he got a wiener dog. Got it at the animal shelter. Cutest little thing Timmy had ever seen. He knew he was supposed to call it a dachshund, but Timmy liked calling him his wiener dog.

He gave him the name of Fred. Fred the wiener dog. Fred had brown fur and a really long belly and short legs with black paws.

He looked like a hot dog. A fat hot dog. Hold the mustard. Hahaha.

Timmy brought Fred with him to the corner. He put him under an umbrella so Fred wouldn't get too hot. He put out a bowl of water and a bowl of food. He wound Fred's leash around the wagon's handle so he wouldn't get loose and run out into traffic and get runned over when Timmy was bringing customers their papers.

Fred only peed on the papers a couple times. He was a good dog, and Timmy loved petting him as much as he could.

AFTER WORK, TIMMY LIKED TO TAKE FRED FOR A walk in the dog park. When either the last paper was sold or it turned noon o'clock, Timmy would howl, "High nooooooooon!"

Fred would join in on the howl. Timmy would howl back. Back and forth they would howl.

"High noooooooon!"

Finally, Timmy couldn't hold off the laughter any longer. He laughed and laughed until his side really hurt.

They'd head for the beach. There, on Atlantic Boulevard, across the street from the beach where kayakers and snorkelers moved through the clean, blue water, Timmy and Fred entered the Higgs Beach Dog Park. It was fenced in, so Timmy could take off Fred's leash and let him run free. There was grass everywhere and benches. It smelled fresh and the ocean breeze cooled them off. At least it cooled off Timmy. Fred never said one way or another. Hahaha.

One day in early December, a girl sort of Timmy's age showed up at the park. With a wiener dog!

Her name was Linda and she was really, really pretty—the girl, not the dog, of course, although Timmy thought all wiener dogs were cute. Linda had a pretty smile and curly dark hair.

She seemed a lot like Timmy. Not that she had a stump for where her right hand was supposed to be. She still had her hand. And she didn't have a scar on her head like Timmy did from the thing that happened in Afghanistan. Timmy even asked her if he could check her hair to be sure, but she didn't.

No scar.

But he still thought she was a lot like him.

Except, of course, for her boobies, but that was because she was a girl. And her hair was long and curly while his was cut very short.

So he supposed they were quite different, but Timmy remained convinced they were almost alike.

"Would you like to meet here again tomorrow?" she asked.

"Sure!" Timmy said. Then added, "I work until noon o'clock, but I'll get here as soon as I can after that."

Timmy almost howled with delight.

EVERY DAY, THEY MET AT THE DOG PARK ON Atlantic. Or arranged to meet at one of the other dog parks. Or just kept the dogs on their leashes and strolled along the trails in the state park.

Timmy liked Linda. A lot.

And she seemed to like him, too.

The wiener dogs seemed to like each other, too. Fred and Charlie.

As the end of the year beckoned, Linda cautiously asked, "Are you doing anything special on New Year's Eve?"

"Oh, no," Timmy said, a pressure suddenly building in his chest. "No, no, no, no, no. Duvall Street is just… just too crazy. Too noisy. The TV cameras and… and too many people. You can't even turn around without bumping into someone!"

Timmy's heart pounded at the very thought.

"It does get crazy," Linda said. "Especially the drag queen in the huge red high heel. Dropping at midnight."

"Yes, people everywhere! Something bad could happen around all those people. Something really bad!"

"But that's at midnight. What about noontime?"

Timmy didn't understand. "Noon o'clock? What about it?"

"Every year at noon on New Year's Eve, there's the wiener dog parade. It's the official start of New Year's Eve."

Timmy felt his jaw drop.

"We could even," Linda said cautiously, "call it a date."

~

The Key West Dachshund Walk began on the corner of Whitehead and Fleming Streets, and would move down to Duvall, the main strip. Traffic had been blocked off all along the way.

Almost all the dog owners had chosen not to dress up at all. They wore the same blouses and T-shirts, ragged shorts, and ratty sneakers as on any other day. The costumes were apparently reserved for the dachshunds.

All three hundred of them.

There were wiener dogs wearing garish sunglasses, superman capes, hot dog buns with fake mustard, leftover Christmas decorations, striped prison suits, and pink tutus. The wiener dogs walked or rode in wagons, baby carriages, pedicabs, or the laps of owners in wheelchairs. There were even dogs of completely different breeds referred to as "honorary dachshunds." A poodle wore a sign that said, "My boyfriend is a dachshund."

And then there were Linda and Timmy, Fred and Charlie, outshining all others.

Timmy wore a dashing white tuxedo with a bright red bowtie. Linda wore a matching bright red, sequined ballroom gown, its straps thin on the shoulders and its lower half billowing out widely.

The costumes were so out of place as to be perfect. Both in the estimation of Timmy and Linda, and the spectators.

The dogs, Fred and Charlie, wore costumes Linda had sewn that matched their owners' garb as closely as possible. This did make Charlie a canine cross-dresser, but this was Key West.

Spectators lining the route broke into applause. Cameras turned their way and did not leave them. Timmy and Linda grinned ear-to-ear. They had spent far too much on these rentals, yet regretted nothing.

Some first dates, they had decided, were worth gambling on.

As he walked down Duvall Street with Linda on his arm and Fred and Charlie at his feet, Timmy felt sure that many of those cheering now were wishing they were him.

And why not? This was the most wonderful moment he could remember. Happiness flooded over him.

He knew he had lost something those years ago in Afghanistan. And chances were, he'd never get it all back. But today—thanks to Linda, Fred, and Charlie—he'd reclaimed some of it.

And maybe together, they could take back even more.

Swipe Left and Guang Gun

Introduction to Swipe Left and Guang Gun

I NEED TO MAKE ONE THING CLEAR UP FRONT before we get to the good stuff. And no, this ain't my version of foreplay.

I worked for thirty-three years writing low-level software for a company manufacturing and selling ultrasound devices all over the world. (That is, until I retired to become a full-time writer, can I hear the "Hallelujah Chorus"?) So I know the ultrasound business. Inside and out.

The point to be made clear? That company never engaged in the illegal and unethical behavior described. Not even close. Never. But the accurate numbers included in this story don't lie. Some company or companies somewhere were profiting greatly from an ethically bankrupt situation.

I'll say no more.

Holy smokes, I've probably got you just about ready to skip this story because you're here for fun and I'm sounding ponderously serious. Please don't. "Swipe Left" is anything but ponderous. In fact, it's loaded with suspense to go along with the romance.

You're gonna like it. Trust me. Or as would-be lovers have so often said, "It's going to be as good for you as it is for me. Maybe even better."

Swipe Left and Gang Gun

Wendy Donahue stepped out of her boss's suddenly claustrophobic office and headed to her cubicle, ears burning and a sour taste in her mouth. The asshat couldn't be serious. She was on track for a "Needs Improvement" rating on her next performance evaluation? Seriously? After fifteen years of almost universally superior marks as a journalist at the *Boston Times*? Never less than "Satisfactory," and even that lukewarm praise coming only three times?

Wendy sat down in her near-microscopic cubicle-for-the-day—first come, first served every morning since the latest round of budget cuts deemed that larger, reserved cubicles were far too lavish an expense—little more than a three-foot-wide desk surface supporting a black phone to the right of her chrome-colored laptop, a notepad, and pen. No photographs or other personal items. An ergonomic nightmare with the laptop, but the bean counters would consider that only after the disability claims rolled in. And if you could lay 'em off before the neck, wrist, and back injuries felled those liabilities-on-the-ledger-sheet known as peon employees, then... *a big win for the stockholders! Yay!*

Could the newspaper business suck any worse? Wendy had always considered herself an optimistic person, but reality had been slapping her down so repeatedly it was hard to still think her cracked, leaking glass was still full.

Needs Improvement? Seriously?

Geez, could it have anything to do with Sandy Sunshine, Wendy's nickname for the intern from Boston University, a blonde cutie with an ass the size of a postage stamp? Definitely a Tinder swipe right. A hard-and-fast swipe right for any man with a pulse. And after graduation this spring, happy to come in at an entry-level salary after working for nothing but "experience" as an intern.

Wendy knew exactly what she herself was. A damned good journalist, forced by the cutbacks to do investigative journalism, her forte, only a fraction of the time. And when it came to Tinder, which she would never bother with in a million years, an automatic swipe left.

Not even a Plain Jane. Drab shoulder-length, dark hair. Drab dark eyes and facial features. A drab thirty-eight years old. Drab, drab, drab.

A Plain Jane *Plus* actually, where Plus stood for Plus-sized clothes since no matter what she tried, she seemed doomed to remain the forty pounds over her doctor's preferred weight she'd carried all the way back to high school when she sat at home for both the Junior and Senior Proms. Learning her lesson at her first dances years earlier where her only dances were with girlfriends who pitied her.

So Wendy poured herself into what she did best. And for fifteen years, that effort and expertise had been recognized. Apparently not anymore.

The phone on her desk rang.

"Wendy Donahue," she answered.

"I have a story for you," a male voice said softly in what sounded like a faintly Asian accent.

Wendy waited for what came next, but the man said nothing. She popped an antacid pill in her mouth and tongued it to the side.

"What kind of story?" she prompted.

The man hesitated, then said, "Could we meet to discuss this? Someplace discreet?"

Wendy never wanted to cut off a source but with other stories to write, she didn't have time to be chasing the equivalent of a PTA bake sale. Was this even worth her while? More importantly, she'd dealt with more than a few nutcases in her time and even had a scar on her left shoulder to prove it. The request for a discreet setting had set off soft alarm bells. Could be legit. Could be the calling card of a nutcase.

"Could you at least give me some idea of what we're talking about?" she asked, sliding the notepad closer and picking up her pen.

The man breathed in deeply. She could all but hear him swallow hard and lick his lips.

"Corporate malfeasance," he said. "Ethically bankrupt and outright illegal. I've done some research on you and read some of your feature stories. You're really good. You're the best person for this."

It's nice the *readers* notice, Wendy thought. Not that the *readers* matter.

The sour taste left by the boss's comments lingered in her mouth despite the antacid tablet, but she pushed all that away.

"Thank you for the kind words," she said. "I'm interested in what you have to say. Where would you like to meet?"

He mentioned an Irish pub in walking distance from the paper's offices. The lunchtime crowd would be long gone so he'd find a booth in the back. In half an hour. He'd recognize her from the photo on the paper's website. He was Chinese and would be wearing a black suit and tie. Name of Jason. No last name. For now.

An hour later, Wendy was wondering if she was falling in love.

For Jason Wu, the wood-paneled boardroom with its long, twelve-person table with him claustrophobically seated in the middle was suddenly oppressively hot, despite the air conditioning.

What was being proposed on the PowerPoint slides displayed on the screen off to his right was wrong. Appalling from both an ethical and legal perspective. It was also personal.

Every eye was on him. Of the dozen SonoLow executives seated around the table, all similarly dressed in dark suits and ties, only he was Chinese. And conspicuously so.

In polite conversation, they referred to him as their Designated China Representative, and indeed he was the only high-level member of the executive team who spoke multiple dialects of fluent Chinese, a necessity to act as the liaison with their partners in Shanghai. Born and raised in China as Chih Hsiang Wu, he came to the United States to attend college, got his green card, and then U.S. citizenship with the Americanized first name of Jason.

He got it that he was special and in many cases, resented, not one of the guys. Special in part because of his unique skills that, combined with an insatiable work ethic that left time for almost nothing else, saw him rise to Vice President of East Asia Sales. But he also knew that he was an outsider in that boardroom, made to feel that he didn't really belong except for his freakish skills useful in a critically huge market. Behind his back, he'd even heard the term Designated China Representative twisted to change "China Representative" into a common slur. And when COVID-19 hit, he faced both open and subtle hostility as if the pandemic was his fault.

So he knew he was on thin ice, unique skills and tireless work ethic or not. He was also smart enough to know he was being asked for his approval, but he really didn't have the option to say no.

"China is our single most critical market," said Kenneth Neilson, Senior Vice President of Marketing and more importantly, the tall, broad-shouldered, good-looking son of the CEO, Clarence Neilson. The son clicked on the next PowerPoint slide displayed on the screen off to Jason's right, a chart with a plummeting line in bright red. "Our drop in revenue there will be catastrophic if it continues. If we don't implement Operation Halcyon Days, the only word we'll need Jason to send to Shanghai will be *sayonara*."

Kenneth shot Jason an icy look, inviting a comment, though clearly only approval would be welcomed.

Jason wasn't going to mention that *sayonara* was Japanese, not Chinese. That was the least of his worries. Operation Halcyon Days was an appalling solution to the admittedly chilling revenue drop.

In his opinion, no solution at all.

SonoLow and its China partner in Shanghai manufactured low-cost ultrasound devices focused on the OB/GYN market. North America and Europe overwhelmingly went for ultra-high-priced premium alternatives from other companies, but SonoLow and its partner dominated East Asia.

Or had at least dominated the region in the recent past.

The halcyon days for the company had taken advantage of China's one-child mandate that decreed that couples were allowed only one child, a policy that extended all the way to 2016. Faced with a hard limit of only one child, families with generation upon generation of biases towards sons over daughters, sought ultrasound images early in a pregnancy to determine the sex of the fetus. The kind of low-cost ultrasound images SonoLow was designed for.

The dirty, unspoken secret was that if the fetus was a female, it was most often aborted. By 2001, 117 boys were born for every 100 girls. SonoLow raked in record profits in China as well as Korea and India, where marriage dowries made female children especially undesirable. Embarrassed by the exposure of the dirty secret and even more concerned about the generation with tens of millions of young men with no available young women to wed, China passed erratically enforced laws against sex-based abortions and eventually sex-based ultrasound tests.

The new laws, combined with the loosening in 2016 to allow two children per couple and then in 2021 to allow three children, were broadsides to SonoLow revenues.

The proposed Operation Halcyon Days would provide a secret combination of bribes to Chinese governmental officials and hospital administrators to allow sex-based ultrasound tests on SonoLow devices and the sex-based abortions that would follow. The sales force of their Chinese partners would also be incentivized to push harder into China's rural areas where the "need" for sex-based ultrasounds and abortions was greater, and oversight more slack.

"So Jason, thumbs up?" asked the younger Neilson.

Jason felt every eye on him. He could either opt for euphemisms or state his mind. Stating his mind could possibly be a fire-able offense, especially since the CEO's prized son was involved.

But sometimes you just had to take a stand.

"This is a mistake," he said, looking first at the senior Neilson at the head of the table. Predictably, he scowled. Jason turned to the son, whose face was flushed and eyes flashed pure hatred.

"And what do you propose to do?" Kenneth Neilson demanded, crossing his arms.

Jason wanted to respond with "not break the law," but instead tried to avoid totally blowing up his career.

"There aren't easy answers right now," Jason said. "But

I believe this proposal would be the equivalent of pouring gasoline on a fire. Breaking the law in China is not the same thing as breaking it here. You can't just get our representatives there a high-priced lawyer and wiggle out of an arrest. You'd be putting our people there in significant danger and breaking laws here as well."

"That's not a solution!" Kenneth Neilson countered.

The senior Neilson wrapped hard on the table. "Let's take a day to cool off and think about it. Especially you, Jason. See if instead of discarding this proposal, you can figure out how it can work."

Jason walked back to his office in a daze. *So it can work? How might that be? Cut the bribes in half?*

Soon after, under the guise of stepping out for a late lunch and having done some quick homework on his personal cell phone, he called Wendy Donahue at the *Boston Times* and arranged to meet at a pub five miles from the office.

He found a dimly lit booth in the back of the pub, around the corner and out of sight from the front door entrance, and surrounded by empty booths.

He only had to wait five minutes for the reporter. When she arrived, he felt a pang of... of *something*. Was it surprise? Awareness? Discomfort?

Attraction? She was no classic beauty by either American or Chinese standards. And yet that had never mattered much to him. Although, what exactly had mattered to him? It had been so long ago and even back then, so pointless. Since then, he'd spent all his time and energy on his career. A career now almost certainly in a shambles.

What he did find attractive was that here was an intelligent woman of great principle. Whose career was spent on exposing evil and righting wrongs. Not just growing, or protecting, market share.

Her own noble career made his feel tawdry by comparison. Especially now that it had led to this ignominious point.

An intelligent woman of great principle. Perhaps those were the most beautiful qualities of all. She hadn't spoken a word in person and yet already...

Jason told himself to snap out of it. This was no romantic rendezvous. If he forgot that for one second, he'd come off as a creep, some kind of a stalker.

This woman and he were here on important business.

And yet...

WENDY SLID INTO THE BOOTH OPPOSITE THE mysterious Jason with no last name. Chinese. Short black hair, neatly combed. About her age. Medium height and weight. Moderately handsome.

Not that she paid attention to that sort of thing anymore. Chinese. White. Black. Short. Tall. Homely. Handsome. Alive. Dead.

Didn't matter. All men had been dead to her for a long time now. Romantically, at least. And that most certainly was *not* what she was here for.

"So," she said, getting right down to the point. "Corporate malfeasance. Ethically bankrupt and outright illegal. You got my attention."

Jason No-Last-Name opened his mouth and then shut it.

A waitress appeared from behind, gave them menus, and asked if they wanted anything to drink.

"Just water," they both said in unison, and gave a brief, almost embarrassed chuckle.

"You want to look at the menu for a minute? It's on me," he said.

The sharp smells of corned beef and cabbage wafted through the air along with beer and whiskey as if to prove this was an authentic Irish pub, but they also mingled with smells Wendy found more appetizing, standard pub fare of mozzarella sticks, cheese fries, and nachos.

"I'm really not that hungry," Wendy said, lying, but wanting to get to business.

"How about I order some nachos? They're good here." He flashed a winning smile. "You can have as much or as little as you'd like. And order anything else you want."

"Suit yourself," Wendy said. "Now about the corporate malfeasance."

Again, Jason No-Last-Name opened his mouth, and again, the waitress appeared. He ordered the nachos. After the waitress noted there would be a two-dollar charge for plate sharing, Wendy caved and ordered the southwest eggrolls.

A worried look came over his face. He leaned closer.

"If I suddenly say to someone, 'Well look who's here!' then please play along," Jason said. "It's someone from work and I can't have them know you're a reporter. You can either be a secret date or some other cover story. Just not a reporter."

"Sounds good," Wendy said, then added with a slight grin, "I'll be a married woman you're having an affair with. Definitely better than talking to a reporter."

Jason nodded, but looked disappointed. "Are you married? I mean, not that it matters." He shook his head. "I'm sorry. Silly question. Forget it."

"Corporate malfeasance?" she said.

"First off, I want you to know that what I am about to say is not anti-abortion. I'm actually pro-choice. But this isn't right."

Wendy felt her face grow hot. Testily, she said, "You brought me here under the guise of corporate malfeasance. Something ethically bankrupt and outright illegal. If you lied to me about that and you're just some abortion nut on *either* side, then I'm leaving now and you *will* pay for what I ordered."

"I'm sorry, I'm sorry, I'm sorry," he said, putting a hand out to ask her to stop, then pulling it quickly back. "That came out all wrong. I don't know what's wrong with me." He shook his head. "This is about ultrasound and sex-based abortions. It's about a corporation trying to circumvent Chinese laws that have been increasingly enforced over the last few years, banning ultrasound scans to determine the sex of the fetus so it can be aborted if it's female."

Wendy felt her jaw drop. She usually maintained a poker face at times like these. It was the professional thing to do. But she couldn't help herself.

"Tell me more," she said.

He told her the whole astounding story, pausing only when the waitress arrived with the nachos and eggrolls. They shared them both, her eating some of the nachos that were, in fact, very good. Crisp with all of the toppings mixed into every layer, not just piled on top, leaving nothing but dry chips underneath. The eggrolls, of which he had one, were also delicious.

He told her his last name. Wu. Jason Wu. Americanized from Chih Hsiang Wu. Then told her about how he'd come to the United States, about his parents back in Shanghai, and about how he'd given up all pretense of a social life to pour his energies into his career.

A career he presumably was blowing up by trying to do the right thing.

Instinctively, Wendy reached out her hand to comfort him. Thoroughly unprofessional. Bewildering. What had gotten into her?

But she felt compassion for the man. Compassion and maybe something more.

Maybe something dangerous.

So when she reached out her hand and touched his, she yanked it back as if it was on fire.

But his reaction was so forlorn when she pulled away that she put her hand back on his. And left it there.

For a long time.

WHEN THE WOMAN, WENDY, PUT HER HAND ON his, feeling his pain, Jason felt his heart melt. *Something* was passing between them. He wasn't sure what it was. He wasn't good at this sort of thing. Actually, he was *awful* at this sort of thing.

He had no experience with women at all.

His generation in China had been one where there were tens of millions of young men like him with no matching woman.

The *guang gun*. The excess males. The ones too poor or too awkward or too... something... to connect with the scarce females who gravitated to others.

And once locked in that path of no relationships, he'd been unable to escape. Even when he got to America, first as a student and then a rising star at SonoLow.

He could not, of course, share that with this wonderful woman. With Wendy.

Wendy, blessed with such beauty of intellect, nobility, and compassion. She had touched his hand and felt his pain without knowing the full extent of it.

The most beautiful woman in the world.

Sadly, they were forced to part. They could not remain forever there at that table in the pub. He still had work to do.

"I believe every word," Wendy said. "But right now, I have no proof. I can't write a story without proof. You need to get me documentation."

"A secret recording of the meeting tomorrow?" Jason asked.

"I'd love to hear it, but I couldn't use it," she said. "Here in Massachusetts, both parties must consent to a recording. So secretly recording that meeting would actually be illegal. You need something on paper."

Wendy headed back to the newspaper office, wondering *what the hell was that?*

While sitting on the keg of dynamite of SonoLow's outrageous shenanigans, what were the two of them doing back in the pub? Half the time acting like love-struck teenagers. Making googly eyes at each other, touching hands, but unable to speak aloud what both of them were probably thinking and feeling.

Probably.

She knew she was feeling something. And with the way Jason had looked at her, he had to be feeling the same thing.

Wendy hoped so.

Jason waited until the administrative assistant who guarded Kenneth Neilson's door left to make photocopies, then knocked on the door.

"Who is it?" the younger Neilson demanded.

"Jason Wu. We should talk."

Silence for several seconds.

"Come in."

The office was larger and more ornate than all but the old man's. A huge mahogany desk. Matching bookshelves on both sides. A floor-to-ceiling glass wall looking out on the Charles River.

Neilson kept him waiting for over a minute as he scanned a folder, a frown lining his brow. Finally, he looked up.

"So?" he said, adding not another word.

"I may have been hasty," Jason said. "I was looking at

the risks, but maybe not enough at the benefits. Could I get your projected numbers so I can run through the cost-benefit analysis? And your PowerPoint slides?"

Neilson hesitated.

"I'm sure you're right," Jason said. "This will just give me the ability to say that tomorrow with confidence."

A smirk came over Neilson's face. He clicked on his computer's mouse a few times, typed a few keystrokes onto his keyboard, then another mouse click.

"On its way," he said.

"Thanks."

"Close the door on your way out."

WENDY MET JASON AGAIN THAT NIGHT AT THE Irish Pub.

"For good luck," Jason had said over the phone. "Same place and I'll try to get the same booth."

Wendy had all but seen his smile as he spoke the words. She finished up at the office and got there five minutes early, but he still beat her.

The place was a bit more crowded, but he'd gotten the same booth and miraculously, the booth closer to the front door and the one angled off to the side were both still empty.

After they placed their order, main courses this time but with the nachos once again as an appetizer "for good luck," Jason placed a light-colored package filled thick with pages on the table. Wendy slid the pages out and began to look at them one-by-one.

"This is perfect," she said. "We can nail them to the wall with this. You did great!"

Jason beamed.

"There is one thing you should be prepared for, however," she said.

"What?"

"We'll wait until this kid Neilson presents tomorrow to make sure you aren't being set up," Wendy said. "Make sure that what he presents matches these numbers. Or is at least close. That will also give me time to clear this with my editor. And he'll want to clear it with Legal, too, because I'm sure the lawsuits will fly. With any luck, this goes to print the day after tomorrow. Online, just after that midnight."

"Great, I'll let you know tomorrow."

"There's one other thing," Wendy said. "It's possible these papers have a special coding or marking that will make it clear that it's your copy that got into my hands. We won't be able to compare it with any other copy to look for differences, but you should be prepared to be identified as my source."

"They'll know it was me anyway."

"They'll fire you," she warned.

"I don't want to work for them anyway."

"This may also put them out of business."

"Good riddance to bad rubbish."

Wendy chuckled softly. "You've thought this all through, haven't you?"

"Yes, I have."

She spread her hands wide. "Then I believe that wraps things up."

Jason smiled and reached behind his back on the booth. He pulled out a single red rose and gave it to her, his hand shaking.

A lump formed in Wendy's throat. For seconds she couldn't speak.

"When this started out, it was supposed to be strictly business," she said, laying the rose flat on the table.

"I'm glad it didn't stay that way," Jason said. "I mean, it didn't, did it? Stay that way?"

"No, it didn't," she said, taking his hand. "And I'm so glad it didn't."

He nodded, looking briefly relieved and then nervous again.

"I also want to tell you why this whole thing with my company—my soon to be former company—is personal," he said.

Wendy nodded. Then she squeezed his hand as he talked of being one of the *guang gun*, the excess males, too poor, unattractive, awkward, introverted, or *something* to attract one of the scarce Chinese young women.

"So I guess you're getting sort of a reject," he said.

Wendy shook her head. "No, never a reject! You are a wonderful person. And I have a few admissions to make myself."

Jason shook his head. "I'll listen to you all night long, but first let me finish with the other reason the ultrasound tests and abortions were so personal to me."

"Okay."

"Remember how I said I was pro-choice. That is true. I believe a woman should have the right to choose. In all cases except perhaps one. I believe it is wrong to get an exam and then abort a fetus solely because it is a girl. I feel that way because I had two older sisters."

Wendy stared at him.

"What would have been my two older sisters, had three children been allowed at that time in China, were both aborted because they were girls. I lived only because they died."

"Oh my," Wendy said.

"I lived so that I could carry on the ancestral name, among other factors. But because I was *guang gun,* I failed that task. I was a bare branch. My mother grew very angry with me when, after I left for the United States, I told her I was staying. She told me then of my older sisters and said that she should have let one of them live and aborted me instead. It couldn't have turned out any worse."

Wendy could think of nothing to say. All she could do was slide out of her side of the booth and slide in with Jason, then wrap her arms around him.

Another time, she would share some of her stories as well. The world had inflicted damage on them both. They would be there for each other to heal the wounds.

Two days later, the *Boston Times* splashed SonoLow's Operation Halcyon Days on the front page. Jason was escorted out of the SonoLow building, fired, even as law enforcement officials arrived for the rest of the executive team.

Wendy's boss conceded that he'd been wrong—a word

previously assumed not to be in his vocabulary—and she was most definitely performing exceptional work.

Wendy and Jason celebrated with a third straight trip—for good luck—to the Irish pub and ordered nachos once again. For good luck.

Afterward, they swore they would never return to the pub or eat nachos again.

They were sick of nachos.

But not each other.

The Forgotten Bach

Introduction to The Forgotten Bach

IF YOU'VE READ MY NOVEL *ROMANTIC CONCERTO for Strings and Brass*, you know of my love for mixing romance with music. (If you haven't read the novel, why not? Give it a try!) In any case, I'm at it again in "The Forgotten Bach."

Unlike *Romantic Concerto*, however, which is set solidly in real-world realism, "The Forgotten Bach" strays into the impossible. So for the second and last time in this volume, I must ask those of you who instinctively wrinkle your nose at the fantastic to indulge me. I trust you found it worth your while with "The Run of Her Life."

How about just this one time more? Pretty please with sugar on it?

You won't be asked to accept trolls, fairies, or goblins. No leprechauns, wizards, or witches. No dragons, were-wolves, or vampires.

Nothing more impossible than a woman transported back almost three hundred years to Germany in the mid-1700s. Just a little time travel.

Piece of cake.

Perhaps you'll agree with readers of this story who are clamoring for more. They want me to turn "The Forgotten Bach" into a novel.

I've got to admit, it's a thought that puts a smile on my face.

<h1 style="text-align:center">The Forgotten Bach</h1>

Trading a total jerk like Willie McNulty for the son of Johann Sebastian Bach was the swindle of a lifetime. See you later, Willie, and don't let the door hit you too hard in your head-stuck-firmly-up-your-ass. Good riddance to bad rubbish.

Marie Doherty wasn't bitter. She was relieved. What could be better than a sitting in a Leipzig café drinking German coffee with whipped cream, looking ahead to a day at the Johann Sebastian Bach Museum, a dinner of *Wiener schnitzel* while sipping ice cold *Weihenstaphaner Hefe Weissbier*, and a Bach concert outside of the twelfth-century St. Thomas church with the great master's statute gazing down upon her.

If Willie hadn't walked out on her practically on the eve of this Trip of a Lifetime, she'd have felt guilty about him not being able to make the trip or felt compelled to compromise every last sightseeing opportunity to appease him.

What had she ever seen in him? The good looks and

aura of success, of course, but that commingled with a need to control her every move and denigrate her own interests. They were a total mismatch, her with a B.A. in Musical History and a minor in Composition, him with a disinterest in anything musical earlier than Eminem. She knew she wasn't particularly pretty, especially the flat chest Willie always complained about and a mostly plain face, and drab, dark hair.

But she could do better. She knew that now. Willie walking out had done her a favor. So now she was free to enjoy Germany on her own, starting at Leipzig.

She finished her coffee and headed for the museum. Outside, across the slate gray exterior, a golden sign read *bach archiv.* She walked through dark wooden doors and made her way through the exhibits. There were busts of all the musical members of the Bach family tree, the master's composing room complete with stained glass windows and a light-colored wooden desk and chair, and atop a white platform, his favorite instrument, an organ and wooden bench.

Marie stood at the organ and imagined one of the three or four greatest composers of all time, sitting on that bench and playing the organ like the virtuoso he was. She brushed her hand across the bench where the genius once sat.

Intoxicated by the sight of the instrument, she stroked the bench with her fingertips. Back and forth. Slowly, as if in a trance, everything except the organ with its white and black keys became cloudy, becoming darker and darker until finally all that remained was the organ and the bench.

Suddenly, the organ began to play all by itself the most exquisite music. A fugue from the Baroque era, Bach's time, but not one Marie recognized and she knew them all. It developed the theme, first in the instrument's soprano, and then the alto, and then the bass.

Slowly, a figure appeared on the bench, playing the fugue, hunched over the keyboard.

Marie pulled her hand away, as if scalded by a hot stove.

She could not believe her eyes.

HEINRICH FELT HELPLESS. ONCE AGAIN. IT WAS his lot in life to be "the feeble-minded Bach."

The embarrassment.

He wondered now, as he had so many other times, if it would have been better for him to have died in infancy or soon thereafter, as had been the case for ten of his siblings. Why had God chosen to take ten of them, as well as Bernhard at the age of twenty-four, while leaving Helpless Heinrich—*Hoffnungsloser Heinrich*—on this Earth to humiliate his father?

Helpless Heinrich, who couldn't attend the school at which his famous father served as Cantor, a position he'd taken largely so that his sons could earn prestigious degrees there. Heinrich's older half-brothers Wilhelm and Emanuel had availed themselves of the education offered and had already established themselves as composers of the first rank.

Not Helpless Heinrich, who was too feeble-minded to attend the school or even copy his father's scores accurately, a task even the least of his father's students could perform with ease. For *Hoffnungsloser Heinrich*, the notes all came out as a mixed-up jumble.

And yet, Heinrich felt music bubbling inside him, even now as he sat at the organ's keyboard in the ten-foot-square room and played the notes he composed within his mind. The music flowed out of him and into his fingers. He felt the beauty of the themes and the variations and the returns back to the themes, felt the splendor of creativity. Surely this was what at least in small measure his father and half-brothers felt.

But when he attempted to transcribe those notes onto a sheet of paper, they became a hopeless mess. And he again became *Hoffnungsloser Heinrich*, Hopeless Heinrich.

A familiar inner rage at his futility boiled once again within him.

Mein Gott! Warum? My God! Why?

A muffled shriek erupted behind him.

Heinrich spun around wide-eyed. There had been no one else in the room when he sat at the keyboard, and even one as feeble-minded as himself would have heard someone enter, even when enraptured in the throes of composing in his mind that which he could not transcribe.

But here was a woman. Dressed in the strangest of clothes. Quite scandalous, in fact. Looking as terrified as he felt.

"*Wer bist du*?" he asked. Who are you?

The woman blinked in a confusion he found strangely attractive, but then replied in the slowest, worst German he had ever heard.

"Mein... Name... ist... Marie," she said.

Anger flashed through Heinrich's entire being. He

might be the feeble-minded son, but he didn't need to be insulted and spoken to like a child or a village idiot.

"*Was ist los mit deinem Deutsch?*" he asked. What is wrong with your German?

"Can you speak English?" the woman asked, her voice quavering.

"Yes, of course. I am not so poorly learned as to not know English." Heinrich frowned. "But this is Leipzig. Why should we speak English?"

"Leipzig," she said, as if absorbing some grand surprise, looking at his dress of a brown vest and knee-length trousers, and his powdered wig as if they were somehow very strange. "I come from afar," she said. "My German is poor. May I ask where in Leipzig this is?" Bowing her head, she asked, "And what is your name?"

Heinrich eyed the strange woman and again felt a strange attraction. Surely it was because, unlike those who knew of his plight, she did look upon him with scorn. A mixture of fear and fascination, but no scorn. It had to be that, he thought. Not that he could actually consider such a strangely dressed woman and one with hardly any bosom at all to be desirable.

And yet.... Heinrich pushed the thought away.

"I am Gottfried Heinrich Bach, son of Johan Sebastian Bach, Cantor of Leipzig," he said. "These are my father's apartments and offices inside the St. Thomas School. Have you become lost? Down the hall are the school's library and classrooms."

The woman's face turned ashen. "What, pray tell, year is this?"

Such an odd question from such an odd woman.

"Why, it is the year of our Lord 1748."

Marie felt as though she might faint. All the rational explanations raced through her mind.

She was dreaming. She was hallucinating. She was going insane.

Her money was on "going insane."

She dismissed that this was a dream. She'd never, ever experienced a dream even close to this vivid. And she'd never taken any drugs at all, not even a puff of weed, and wouldn't resort to aspirin unless a headache or some malady was about to send her to bed. She'd never once hallucinated.

Which left insanity. Hardly an attractive option. But what else was there? That somehow by stroking the organ bench in the Bach Museum she'd slipped all the way back to 1748, two years before Johann Sebastian Bach's death, an event that heralded the end of the Baroque Era, and she was now talking to one of Bach's sons?

Marie supposed that the mental clarity to pinpoint herself two years before the legendary composer's death and speaking with an almost totally forgotten son dictated that this was no hallucination. Her mental faculties were still with her, albeit hardly tested by details she'd learned years ago.

So what was this? She had absolutely no idea, but it would be best to roll with the punches and see where they took her.

"Could you play that music again, the music you were

performing when I arrived?" she asked. "I found it most interesting. A fugue and yet not one of your father's that I recognized."

Heinrich beamed. "It is my own composition."

"Really?" Marie said. "I thought it was wonderful." For the briefest moment, disbelief that such intricate beauty could have been composed by the mentally deficient Bach passed through her mind, but then she rejected it. She recalled in the deepest recesses of her education that his older half-brother—had it been Carl Philipp Emanuel?— had claimed that Heinrich was actually, at least at one point, a great genius who had somehow failed to develop. She asked, "Could you play it again?"

The proud smile on Heinrich's face faltered.

"I will do my best," he said. "But I have never recorded it on paper. I play only from my memory, and only my father's abilities in such matters would allow a perfect rendition of what you heard before."

Marie was astonished. "But why have you never recorded it on paper?"

Heinrich flushed. "Shall I play it for you or shall we chatter like old women?"

Marie felt herself redden. "Play it for me. Please."

As the complex polyphony of Heinrich's fugue filled the air, Marie could not take her eyes off of him. As the organ sounded its notes, she felt her own heart strings being plucked. He was an attractive man, notwithstanding the powdered wig which would take some getting used to, but with broad shoulders and a pleasing, if somewhat haunted, smile.

And while no one in the twenty-first century composed

fugues, there was no denying the beauty of this piece and the creativity of its author.

When he finished, she applauded heartily.

"Bravo! Wonderful!" she cheered.

Heinrich beamed with pleasure. "Would you like to hear another composition of mine?"

"Of course!" Marie said. Though he'd seemed touchy about his failure to transcribe the first piece, she couldn't resist asking the question that begged for an answer. She could no more remain silent than a man dying of thirst could turn down a glass of water.

"Forgive me for asking," she said, "but is this next one also unrecorded?"

His face darkened. "All of my compositions are unrecorded," he snapped.

"But why?"

He glared angrily at her but said nothing.

"Don't you want to record them for posterity?" she asked, and winced as soon as the words were out of her mouth.

"For posterity? Whyever would I do that?"

Marie wanted to kick herself. She'd known the answer to that question intellectually, but in her amazement of actually being here had fumbled and asked anyway. Composers of this era did not envision writing pieces for posterity.

"I meant, so that your pieces could be published and shared in other cities and towns in Germany and perhaps in other countries."

"Do you mock me?"

"No! Your music should be heard far beyond these walls!"

Heinrich looked at her sullenly. He appeared to be weighing an important decision.

"Because you have come from afar, you have not heard of my affliction," he said. "I have been cursed so that I can neither play the notes I see on a page nor record the notes I play. I have the musical knowledge, but when I play what is on the page or record what I play, the notes are all out of order and out of place." He looked down at the floor. "The son of the great Bach cannot even read music."

Marie's jaw dropped. *He's dyslexic! Dyslexia extends to music as well!* Heinrich was no more feeble-minded than anyone else. In fact, based on what she'd heard, he was brilliant.

"Would you allow me to record your composition?" she asked.

IT WAS PAINSTAKINGLY SLOW AS HEINRICH played the passages over and over for the woman to record every note and then verify it since he could not. With anyone else, he would have lost patience. But somehow looking upon this woman's face bestowed a patience on him he'd never known. Her eyes intently watching him play— *loving his music!*—a lock of her hair falling over one eye. An inexplicably attractive scent upon her of roses and lavender.

Heinrich belatedly wondered about the impropriety of it all. Where had this woman come from? And what were these seductively tight garments that she wore. The two of them should not be here together alone without a chaperone.

It was highly improper. Scandalous.

But he enjoyed her presence, and not just her delight at his music, which was nectar of the gods all by itself. For him to be other than the source of ridicule filled his breast with warmth. But even more than that, her presence was an intoxication that threatened to make him light-headed.

His heart sank.

As a feeble-minded man, he could not in good conscience entertain thoughts of a future with this woman. Strange as she may be with peculiar customs and an independence that bordered on the scandalous all by itself, she should never be burdened with a union with him that would produce feeble-minded children.

He must never marry.

Heinrich was resigned to that fate until she looked up after transcribing a particularly complex sequence and said, "This is brilliant! You are brilliant!"

The words warmed his heart and then cut him to the quick because he knew they could not be true.

Filled with sadness, he said, "I am but a feeble-minded man—"

"No," Marie said, shaking her head insistently. "You aren't feeble-minded at all. You are brilliant. I believe you suffer from what people in my land call *dyslexia*."

"I've never heard of such a thing."

"It's only become understood quite recently," she said. "I'm no expert and there's no cure, but I believe there are things that can be done to help you."

Heinrich took it all in. For a time, he could not speak or move or barely even breathe.

Hope flooded over him. And with that hope came the urge to take Marie in his arms and hold her close.

Marie stared into Heinrich's slate gray eyes and wondered if he was feeling for her what she was feeling for him. Not her admiration for his talent, creativity, and astounding resilience to persevere in the face of being deemed feeble-minded when the exact opposite was the case. She couldn't admire that enough. But her heart had somehow leaped across almost three hundred years and been captured by this man.

Did he feel that, too?

He seemed to answer by reaching out a hand and taking hers in his.

"I would like you to meet the rest of my family at dinner tonight," he said.

Marie smiled and said, "I'd love that."

It was hard to see exactly where the light at the end of this tunnel would be.

Was she stranded here in 1748? This was an era without modern medicine and she'd studied enough of Germany in this era to know that a woman's role in society was summed up by the three K's: *Kinder* (children), *Kirche* (church), and *Küche* (kitchen). That would not do for her.

Johann Sebastian Bach would also die in two years and without her, Heinrich would go to live with his married sister, Liesgen, until his own death. His mother would have to live off charity and money sent by a son and eventually die in poverty and be buried in a pauper's grave.

Other than Heinrich, 1748 didn't appear attractive at all.

Could she return to her own era and bring Heinrich with her? He'd have to deal with mind-boggling changes.

Could they go back and forth, like retirees from New England spending the winters in Florida only to return every Spring?

Marie didn't have all the answers. In fact, she had none of the answers except for one. It was expressed in the hand holding hers.

She didn't know where their happily ever after would take place. Only that there would be a happily ever after and it would be with each other, filled with the sweetest of music.

Cape Cod Chips and the Goggles Guy

Introduction to Cape Cod Chips and the Goggles Guy

WHEN I WROTE THIS STORY, IT WAS MY FINAL YEAR of juggling a demanding daytime software engineering job, teaching either two or three evenings a week at local universities, covering college hockey six months a year, and writing fiction.

Yeah, an insane schedule.

My daughter and son by this time were on their own, adults without the need for their dad's daily guiding hand. And Brenda, The Best Wife Ever™, was, as always, outrageously supportive.

Still, an insane schedule, and one I'd been maintaining for a very long time.

It would be my final season of twenty-four years covering college hockey, and two years later I would also retire from the software engineering day job, both retirements to allow more time for fiction writing, my number one passion (outside of family). Nonetheless, this story came while I was still knee deep, or more accurately, way in over my head, in an insane schedule that required more hours than existed in a day.

As a result, time after time, I'd paint myself into a corner with seemingly no way out. Impossible deadlines loomed, some of them feeling mutually exclusive. Invariably, though, with extraordinary intensity, every last bit of brainpower I could muster, and Brenda's support, I'd extricate myself Houdini-like from that impossible, self-made trap.

After many such hair-raising escapes, I'd take a deep breath to calm my pounding heart and nerves, shake my head in that time-honored, self-loathing gesture that asks why-do-I-do-this-to-myself, then give a wry grin to Brenda and say, "Thank God I'm brilliant."

We'd laugh and wonder how long it would be before I found myself yet again in such an impossible circumstance, knowing full well the answer was "soon." Maybe not tomorrow or next week, but soon. It was inevitable.

With my writing, I always tried to limit the painting of myself into a corner to plot complications that don't have an obvious way out. (If I surprise myself in how my characters escape, so, too, are you, kind reader. A win for us both.) I try to respect writing deadlines and not cut it too close.

Sometimes, though, my writing subconscious has other ideas—*deadline? what deadline?*—or those outside pressures from the real world paint me into the corner whether I like it or not, and it becomes a challenge to both write the best possible story I can write and also hit the deadline. Houdini Hendrickson somehow pulls it off more often than the insufferable nitwit deserves.

But not this time. This time, Houdini needed help.

In January of 2020, WMG Publishing sent out a call for the Valentine's Day equivalent of its *Holiday Spectacular* advent calendar of Winter holiday fiction. Edited by the extraordinary writer Annie Reed, the *Valentine's Spectacular* would feature eight romance short stories sent to subscribers one each day leading up to February 14.

Sign me up! Both as a reader and a writer.

Almost immediately, I conceived of what I thought was a pretty good launching pad for the story: two contestants in a Valentine's Day triathlon, mixing it up in... well... I will divulge no spoilers. You'll find out soon enough.

I thought this setting would distance itself from that of other writers—no "low-hanging fruit" here of obvious ideas adopted by countless others—and would appeal to my own interests. Weeks earlier, I had completed my first marathon and was branching off into triathlons, an endeavor that would lead to me completing my first Half Ironman triathlon (aka Ironman 70.3) in the summer of 2023.

Writing this story promised to be great fun. And it was. I even pestered my niece Cherie Hendrickson, a veteran Ironman, for even more details I hadn't yet encountered firsthand. (Thank you, Cherie!)

Great fun. Until the deadline loomed: Sunday, midnight, Pacific Time.

Uh-oh. Houdini Hendrickson was still stuck in the corner. The deadline—3:00 a.m. my time on the East Coast —was a hard one. No exceptions. Even for Houdini. If the email submission arrived at 3:01 a.m. or later, it would be deleted, unread.

The minutes ticked down and the ending simply...

did... not... work. I loved the story, but it was falling flat on its face *so close to the finish line I could taste it*. I could all but lick the bitter blood off my lips caused by my beloved story's faceplant.

I fixed the ending as best I could, the rough equivalent of applying a Band-Aid on a gushing wound, and pressed "send" on the email at precisely 2:50 a.m. (Don't believe me? Come over the house sometime, and I'll show it to you in my email "sent" folder.) It wasn't the first time this clown had cut it so close. My most famous story, "Death in the Serengeti," had been a 2:54 a.m. submission. But in every other pushing-the-time-limit case, I'd been happy with the story I sent. It had been as good as I could make it.

Not this time. This time, I'd blown it. With a few more hours, I could have done better than drag that story's battered and beleaguered body across the finish line. The story could have, should have, raced across the line, strong and victorious. Not get dragged helplessly across.

I hated myself.

Filled with self-loathing that I hadn't pulled off the ending the story deserved—why hadn't I somehow carved out more time earlier in the week to avoid this disappointment?—I headed off to bed and tried to get to sleep. After all, the day job beckoned in just a few short hours. And perhaps a class to teach that night until 9 p.m. as well. Best get some sleep. I'd need it.

But who cared? Certainly not me. I deserved to sleep-walk through the next day, feeling miserable. I'd blown it. I wasn't Houdini Hendrickson. I was Dumbass Dave.

A few months later, though, Annie Reed rode to my rescue. With editors and writers gathered to discuss submitted stories at WMG's Anthology workshop, Annie noted the unsatisfying ending but then gave me a second chance with the most magical of words.

"Will you write me another ending that makes me believe these two are going to have a romance?" Annie asked.

I all but jumped out of my skin. I responded with an exuberant, euphoric yes.

Annie Reed, my hero. She gave me that second chance, and I'd like to think I made the most of it.

"Cape Cod Chips and the Goggles Guy" became the opening story emailed to *Valentine's Spectacular* subscribers. A year later, when the stories were collected into an electronic and print anthology, it became the closing story. Two honored positions for a story. The first convinces a reader to keep reading; the last convinces her to buy the next book.

Yeah, I love this story.

Cape Cod Chips and the Goggles Guy

WHAT DO YOU DO FOR VALENTINE'S DAY WHEN you've given up on men? For Sheila Winston the answer was simple: compete in an Ironman Triathlon. Swimming for 2.4 miles, cycling for 112 miles, and then running a full marathon of 26.2 miles, all within the absolute limit of seventeen hours, was like Club Med compared to her past relationships.

She stood with two thousand other triathletes packed on the beach of Lake Richard, an hour outside of Orlando, Florida, thirty abreast stretching back from the starting line at the water's edge. Sand sifted between her toes. The air hung heavy with humidity.

Sheila double-checked her goggles for a tight fit, then pulled her gold-colored, latex cap down over her hair and the goggle straps, making sure it was smooth against her scalp for the least amount of water resistance. All the competitors wore wet suits; hers was black with red lettering across the chest and sleeveless, exposing the inch-and-a-half, black numerals 1793 on her biceps.

She shrugged her shoulders and shook her arms. She craned her neck to one side and then the other. Her heart pounded with excitement and sheer terror. This was her first time attempting a full Ironman triathlon, the Mt. Everest of endurance events. And yet despite the terror she tried to hide, this still beat yet another teary-eyed breakup with yet another self-absorbed jerk who thought he deserved better than her, and she should be happy he blessed her with his presence.

At least the breakups had sure felt that way.

Time after time.

In the old days, Sheila the Mouse had overlooked the selfish attitudes, the inconsiderate behavior, and the petty slights. She gave and didn't require any taking in return; she just kept giving, hoping that someday, with somebody, it would be appreciated.

It wasn't. Not really.

When a boyfriend commented on her admittedly miniscule breasts, comparing them to mosquito bites, Sheila the Mouse apologized for what God had chosen not to give her. She read the women's magazines and obsessed over losing the extra ten pounds she perpetually carried, then blamed her obviously flawed character when the pounds either wouldn't go away or came back with a vengeance, adding a few more in an extra blow to her psyche. She attempted new hairstyles to breathe excitement into her shoulder-length, jet-black hair that just hung there limp and lifeless no matter what she did.

All to no avail.

And she would have died that way four years ago at the ripe old age of twenty-five due to a previously undiagnosed heart abnormality if not for her cardiac arrest coincidentally coming a mere twenty feet away from a nurse who could keep Sheila alive with fifteen minutes of CPR.

She emerged from the resulting open-heart surgery with a zipper scar down the middle of her still unimpressive chest, running from a few inches below her throat down to almost the base of her ribs.

Even more importantly, though, she emerged with her inner mouse slayed, replaced with a roaring lion. She'd come close to dying before she'd really started to live. She sure as Shinola wasn't going to get cheated after being given a second chance. She would be nobody's doormat. She would kick asses and take no prisoners.

As soon as she was back on her feet, she threw out her mooch of a boyfriend who was never going to get a job no matter what he said. He was never even going to try, and was quite possibly cheating on her anyway.

Gone. See you later. Don't let the door hit you too hard in the ass.

And when his successors took the first steps of walking all over her, they were gone, too. Don't tell me you're sorry. You showed yourself for what you really are.

Good.

Bye.

And when the last and final jerk of jerks had asked her to keep her blouse on while they made love—"your chest and that zipper scar are kind of, you know, a turnoff"—she gave him the heave ho and resolved not to waste any more time on the male species.

Sheila dove into everything else, living life for all it was worth, doing nothing halfway. She quit her dead-end, commute-from-hell job in downtown Boston and took a chance—*took a chance!*—on opening a new business of her own. With a new appreciation for the fragility of life, she embarked on an exercise program, finding her sweet spot in triathlons. With the approval of her cardiologist, she took on first the shortest variation, a sprint triathlon, then moved to the Olympic distance, and then a Half Ironman in which all the distances were half the full torture chamber.

Which brought her here to the Lake Richard beach on Valentine's Day, both thrilled and terrified at the same time, with a cheering squad of zero, which was just the way she liked it.

She was, however, taking a strategic page out of her old Sheila the Mouse playbook. She hung back in the last row of all the triathletes and on the far left. Not to stay out of the limelight, but because the one thing that did spook her out was the free-for-all into the water at the start of the race. The tiniest bit of the mostly banished Old Sheila did pop out of her mouse hole and twitched its whiskers at the thought of everyone crashing into and elbowing each other as they raced into the water, packed like sardines in a can.

The inadvertent kicks to the head. The knocking askew of her swim goggles. Even a swimmer from behind swimming right over and on top of her before he realized what he was doing. And the resulting gulp not of air but of muddied water. It had all happened to her once or twice in her three years of racing, building up to this, her first Ironman.

So she really wasn't being a mouse, she told herself. It was a smart strategy to be one of the last ones into the water. Your personal clock didn't start until you crossed the starting line. You remained at 0:00 while the other sardines in the can thrashed about. Why not give yourself a less crowded first few minutes of your swim? Not because she was still a mouse. Just smart strategy.

And so the gun went off and the elites crashed into the water in their own separate wave, followed by the rest of them. The rows of swimmers inched forward toward the starting line, bit by bit, until finally, Sheila was there.

With her once-cardiac-arrested heart pounding, she stepped over the starting line, triggering the timing chip strapped onto her left ankle, then splashed into the muddy water. In no time, she was passing slower swimmers, weaving in and out of the openings between them.

She never saw the guy cutting diagonally across her path until it was too late.

BRIAN O'CONNELL WAS IN A GROOVE. SANDY haired and well built—six feet tall and one hundred eighty pounds beneath his green swim cap and black-and-red wet suit—he cut through the water smoothly and powerfully, at least according to the mental images playing as he swam.

Reach with the left arm, kick with the right leg. Reach with the right arm, kick with the left leg. Breathe. Reach, kick, reach, kick, breathe.

Rinse and repeat.

A year ago, in this same race, he had failed to make the swimming cutoff of two hours and twenty minutes. A minute and half past the required threshold, he was not allowed to continue. He had failed before even getting to cycling, his strongest sport by far, one where he could make up considerable time. He never got a chance to find out how much.

Stick a fork in him. He was done.

His parents and three members of his triathlon team had flown from Boston to cheer him on and soak up some Florida sun. Brian had had to face them all.

A failure.

He hadn't even mounted his bike. Which had cost almost three hundred dollars just to ship down here.

So this year he'd paid for underwater videotape analysis of his stroke, and put in even more pool time. He'd then made the difficult request of his parents and friends that they not come and see him. He couldn't bear to face them if he failed yet again. Better that he fail alone than reprise last year's sad scene.

Not that he was going to fail. Brian hadn't put all that effort into improving his swimming only to fall short. He was going to make the swimming cutoff, then use his cycling skills to give himself enough of a buffer for the run to squeak in under seventeen hours.

It would be close. Finish in seventeen hours *and two seconds*, and you'd be listed officially as a DNF.

Did Not Finish.

Determined to avoid that gut-wrenching result, Brian had positioned himself on the beach in the middle of the pack, splashed into the water, dealt with an early kick in the head, and gotten into his rhythm.

Reach, kick, reach, kick, breathe. Reach, kick, reach, kick, breathe.

When he neared the third of five giant tomato-red buoys bearing the Ironman logo—clear through Brian's custom prescription goggles—two minutes ahead of his goal time, Brian gave a mental fist pump. He was going to do it!

Reach, kick, reach, kick, breathe.

He was going to do it!

Until—

A hand clouted him across the top of the head. Then a body swam over him—a female body—and kicked him in the head.

Water flooded into his goggles. And then—

They were gone!

Either ripped from his head or the strap had broken.

Brian blinked, saw the glitter of the goggles' reflective surface several feet down. In a panic—*he couldn't lose his goggles!*—he dove.

He stretched for the goggles and—*thunk!*—his head crashed into another swimmer's. A wide-eyed woman who was also stretching out for the goggles. The same one who had presumably just run him over. Number 1793 according to the inch-and-a-half-sized, black markings on her right bicep.

From behind, another swimmer crashed into him.

By the time he righted himself, the goggles were gone. Swimmer 1793 apparently didn't see them either. After pushing away a swimmer that crashed into her, she spread her arms in a palms-up, don't-know gesture, yelled out, "Sorry!" and was off.

No goggles! Brian ducked underwater again, but for all he could tell, his goggles were down on the floor of the lake, embedded in the weeds or whatever made up the darkness down there.

Lost and gone forever. As, of course, was his chance of making the cutoff and being allowed to continue the race.

He was finished. Again.

Stick a fork in him. Again. He was done. Again.

SHEILA FELT AWFUL, BUT WHAT COULD SHE DO? The guy had lost his bearings and cut diagonally across her path and those of the other swimmers around her. She might have seen him coming if she were a left-side breather or even breathed bilaterally—from both sides—but she breathed only from the right and never saw him until the collision.

She mentally wished him luck and darted past other swimmers whose forms were less streamlined than her own, or whose stroke cadences were slower.

Reach and elongate her body. Reach and elongate.

She finished in an hour and fifty-six minutes, staggered out of the water, unzipped her wet suit, and let her designated "stripper" pull it off her. Sheila tucked it under her arm and raced for the transition area where her bike and supplies waited. She took her gear bag from a thin, gray-haired, sixtyish woman with glasses, and ducked into the female changing tent. Even as a woman next to her stripped naked and put on all dry clothes, Sheila kept her triathlon shorts on—they'd dry fast enough—changed into her neon yellow shirt, and put on sunscreen, her sunglasses, her

Garmin race watch, and then her bike shoes, ratcheting them tight.

She raced to her bike—the shoes and cleats awkward for running but not impossible—slipping on her helmet as she went. She ran the bike past the mount line, clipped in, and was off.

Two hours later, she heard a voice from behind bellow out her number.

"Hey, 1793!"

BRIAN WAS NOT A QUITTER. BUT HE'D NEVER, EVER swum in competition without his goggles. All those extra hours spent in the pool to help him make this cutoff time had, of course, been with goggles. The last time he'd been in a pool or a lake without goggles would have been back when he was a ten-year-old at summer camp.

You just couldn't swim competitively without goggles. You needed open eyes to see where you were going, and the human eye was not designed to see under water.

But what was he going to do, quit? That would be an even more ignominious end than the year before.

So he'd give it his best shot. And if miracle of miracles, he did make the cutoff, he was going to chase down number 1793 and give her a piece of his mind.

With that number burning inside him, Brian clenched his eyes tightly shut and began to stroke, opening his eyes only briefly when he lifted his head to find his blurry target.

1793!

Reach, kick. Reach, kick.

1793!

In a miracle that felt on par with the 1980 US Olympic Hockey team defeating the Russians, Brian beat the two-hour, twenty-minute cutoff by thirty-three seconds.

He headed for the Transition area, where his glasses and 20-20 vision awaited him, with only one thing on his mind.

1793!

As she cycled along the far right side of the blocked-off, two-lane roadway, Sheila licked her lips and dreamed of the Cape Cod potato chips awaiting in her special needs bag at mile sixty. Even when not racing, she considered the chips out-of-this-world delicious. When racing, though, they became magical. She craved their salt on her tongue.

But that was still many miles away. She popped a salt tablet into her mouth and squeezed half of a banana-raspberry energy gel pack into her mouth. She washed it all down with Gatorade from her front bottle.

Sheila rested her arms on the aero bars that lowered her body to be more parallel to the ground to reduce wind resistance. The good thing about triathlons in the heat—and today it was in the high seventies and humid—was that the hottest time of the day came while on the bike with the cooling air flowing past you. And Florida simply didn't have a lot of hills. So far, the course had been exceptionally flat.

Not that that made the stiffness in her back any easier to take, nor the growing soreness in her butt. Human beings were not meant to spend seven or eight consecutive hours on a racing bike seat. And Good Lord, she could use some Cape Cod chips right now. She could taste the salt of her sweat on her lips. When she swiped sweat off her forehead, she felt the grainy texture of the salt her body was pumping out of her. Salt stains covered her neon shirt's sweat rings.

She needed more salt to avoid cramping. And she was barely a third of the way into the bike course. She wasn't sure she was going to make it.

"*Hey, 1793!*" a male voice from behind bellowed.

She glanced quickly back, but gave it only a glance. Not paying attention was a good way to crash and get hurt. He was about eight cycle-lengths behind her.

"*Hey, 1793!*"

Sheila didn't bother turning around this time. It was the Goggles Guy, she could tell. Were Prime-A Jerks destined to follow her wherever she went? Even on an Ironman triathlon bike course?

He called out again. Over her shoulder, she yelled, "*What?*"

There was no drafting in these races. That was purely for the professionals. Each rider had to maintain at least a six cycle-length gap from the bike in front, or if passing on the left, had only twenty-five seconds to pull ahead and then complete the pass. Failure to adhere to those rules would result in a time penalty. So the Goggles Guy couldn't get much closer than he'd already been when she'd last glanced back, and he couldn't pull beside her and berate her for the incident.

Sure enough, he called out, "On the left!" and began his charge. In seconds, he pulled alongside and, following the rules, continued past.

But before he left her in his wake, he yelled out, "Pay attention next time!"

Sheila, who no longer suffered fools gladly, yelled back, "Learn how to swim straight!"

He slowed for a split second, and then continued on, picking up the pace even more.

She didn't see him again until mile eighty-seven, well after the replenishment from her special needs bag and the magical Cape Cod chips. He was fixing a flat tire on the side of the road.

Sheila felt compassion for him until he shot her what appeared to be a dirty look. Oh, really? Well, if that was how he wanted to play the game, she could play it that way, too.

A dollop of schadenfreude would *not* be enough.

As she passed him, Sheila pointed to his flat tire and called out, "Is that my fault, too?"

Brian wasn't going to say a word when he caught and passed the woman for a second time. He was just going to look her way in stony silence.

But when she mockingly blew him a kiss, he couldn't help but laugh. It was a funny move. Even in these circumstances.

So he replied, "Happy Valentine's Day!"

Then left her in the dust.

SHEILA FELT LIKE A PRISONER WHO'D BEEN SET free when she finally pulled into T2, the transition area between the bike and run. She'd already unstrapped her bike shoes while still moving into the area, and had stood on her pedals for much of the previous mile just to give her butt a rest and straighten out her stiff back.

If there was a hell, it was to spend an eternity sitting on a racing bike seat.

She changed into her running shoes, wolfed down two bananas and of course, some Cape Cod chips, washed them down with Gatorade, then headed off for the final 26.2 miles of her quest.

Her legs felt like jelly, as if she'd stepped off a boat that had been out to sea for weeks. She wobbled unsteadily, but pushed herself onward. To her surprise, she found herself thinking of the Goggles Guy.

"Happy Valentine's Day!" he'd shouted in response to her blown kiss, much to her amusement.

She realized that she'd been spending a lot of time thinking about him. Why? She couldn't say. Initially, there'd been some anger borne out of their confrontation, but she felt compassion for his plight. To both lose your goggles *and* have to fix a flat tire was getting dealt a very bad hand indeed. But what Sheila felt wasn't just pity.

A sense of dread came over her. She couldn't possibly be falling down the rabbit hole of attraction for a good-looking man yet again, could she? Would she never learn her lesson?

But if she wasn't falling down that rabbit hole—hell, if she wasn't already all the way down the damned thing— then why had she spent so many miles thinking about him? How had she already figured from just a few glimpses that he was about her age, six feet tall, and athletically built?

Why did his "Happy Valentine's Day!" response to her mocking blown kiss put such a smile on her face? Because she'd always been a sucker for guys with a sense of humor?

Good Lord, it was happening again. Even after she'd sworn she was done, done, done with men. *Finis. Kaput.* Shoot me if I ever let a jerk into my heart again.

And it was happening during the third stage of an Ironman triathlon. How pathetic was that?

Time to get the Goggles Guy out of her mind before he got any further into her life. Time to focus on completing the race in under seventeen hours.

It was going to be tight. Roughly two hours for her swim and seven-and-a-half for the bike. That left another seven-and-a-half for running the marathon, which had seemed achievable while she was training. Just average seventeen minutes a mile, mixing running with power-walking. A piece of cake unless you'd already swam over two miles, cycled a hundred and twelve, and your legs felt like jelly.

Please God, not a DNF. Did Not Finish.

She'd trained too hard and too long to either get pulled from the course before the end, or reach the finish line but too late to be official.

As the miles crept slowly by, darkness and temperatures fell and Brian had a tougher and tougher time convincing his legs to run. Even as pockets of spectators lined the blocked off roads and cheered, his legs felt heavy.

So very heavy.

He'd stopped to get a PowerBar and Gatorade at the mile nine aid station when the woman, number 1793, and her neon yellow shirt emerged from the darkness. She was still running.

Just what he needed!

But she smiled his way and repeated his quip. "Happy Valentine's Day."

It was a nice smile, he had to admit. A really, really nice smile. And that blown kiss of hers was the action of a strong woman with a helluva sense of humor.

He found both attractive.

He realized, even with his body drained of every last ounce of energy, he was *smiling* back at her.

Seriously? *Smiling?*

She grabbed a PowerBar, some gel packs, and a Gatorade and began to powerwalk, striding long and purposefully. She looked back at him with what he thought might actually be affection of some kind. Strangely enough, he found himself returning it.

What was he doing?

"Gotta get moving," she said. "Seventeen more miles."

Brian's shoulders slumped. *Seventeen.* Might as well be a hundred. He was totally out of gas. "I don't know if I can make it."

She looked about to turn and leave, but then stopped. "You didn't quit when you lost your goggles. You didn't quit when you got the flat tire. You're going to quit now?"

Brian felt blood rush to his face. "No."

"Then follow me." And she was off, running again.

Not sure that he wanted to, Brian followed, barely managing to stay within fifteen or twenty yards behind her, her neon yellow top glowing like a beacon in a darkness broken only by the roadside streetlights.

He thought about that saucy, sassy blown kiss. About that killer smile.

It had to be oxygen deprivation. There was just no way he could be falling for a woman in his current state, much less someone who'd knocked his goggles off.

Even if she'd tried to retrieve them. Even if she'd yelled out, "Sorry!" Even if he'd maybe, just maybe, caused the collision himself.

What? Now he was taking the blame for the collision?

Definitely oxygen deprivation.

Even so, he found himself forcing his legs to move to stay within sight of her. Keeping his eyes focused on the back of her bright neon yellow top. And yes, a few glances a bit lower to her shorts. And to those athletic legs.

Not in a sexist-caveman kind of way. That wasn't him. It was in a boyfriend kind of way.

Brian blinked. *A boyfriend kind of way?*

Seriously? Where did that come from?

Yes, seriously.

Wow.

He had to keep up with her because he somehow knew that if she took off and he lost sight of her and the pleasing bounce of her black hair on her shoulders and the athletic strength of her stride, he would never find her at the finish line.

And never see her again.

So he stayed as close as he could in the darkness, pushing himself even though he seemingly had nothing left with which to push. His spirits brightened like a silly teenager whenever she passed beneath a roadside streetlight and he could see her better.

And when she slowed to briefly powerwalk at mile eighteen, he caught up and they walked side-by-side, their exhaustion limiting them to only a few words but enough to realize they both lived in suburbs around Boston.

Then after a silence that felt all too short, Sheila looked at her watch and announced, "We've gotta run."

Brian groaned inwardly. He felt as though this was Jupiter. The gravity was crushing him. Everything hurt. "Don't know if I can."

"You want to DNF?"

"Hell, no."

"Me neither. So get the lead out." And once again, she was off.

Once again, Brian couldn't keep up with Sheila, but he also wouldn't let himself lose sight of her. The neon top. The hair bouncing on her shoulders. Even as his legs quivered and his entire body felt wrung out like an old, damp rag, he pushed himself onward.

He would not lose this woman.

SHEILA WANTED TO HELP BRIAN, BUT SHE HADN'T trained for endless hours for several years just to throw it all away on a total stranger. Even one she'd fallen for in a near instantaneous tumble down the rabbit hole of love.

Her eyes widened. *Love?* Had she really thought that word? What the hell was wrong with her? She was willing to admit *attraction*, even amidst the sweat and grime of an Ironman, but no, no, no to the L-word.

And an absolute no to allowing him to take down both of their Ironman dreams, like a drowning man also dragging his potential rescuer to a watery grave. And by mile twenty-three, Brian seemed to be drowning with the potential of taking her down, too.

"We're cutting it too close," she called over her shoulder, belatedly realizing that except when she powerwalked, he seemed only capable of staying close to her. When she slowed down, so did he. When she slowed down even more, he followed suit. The only way she could get him across the finish line in time—get them both across the finish line in time—was to force him to pick up the pace or lose her.

So she did.

Tough love.

The L word again! Was her brain failing as badly as her stiff-as-a-board back, quads, hamstrings and every other aching, cramping muscle in her body? It had to be!

Pushing all thoughts of the L-word aside, she called out, "Stick with me and I'll get you home!"

BRIAN ALMOST CRIED OUT IN AN AGONY THAT WAS both physical and mental. Here in the suddenly chilly darkness, his muscles were shutting down on him. He wanted so badly to sit down for just one minute.

Just one sweet, blissful minute.

But he also knew that if he sat down, he'd never get up. So he had to keep moving. And not just moving. He had to keep up with Sheila. He couldn't lose her.

Couldn't.

But he didn't think he could keep up. And that would mean jeopardizing not only his Ironman dreams, but even worse, Sheila's.

Even worse? Yes, even worse. He couldn't allow her to fail because of him. He couldn't drag this remarkable, fascinating woman down with him.

He had to move his failing legs not just for him, but for her, too. Especially for her.

SHEILA NEARED THE TWENTY-SIX-MILE ROADSIDE banner. Only two-tenths of a mile to go. The cheering of the crowd at the finish line—so close now!—grew louder and louder, replacing her waves of fatigue with exhilaration and adrenaline. Her dream was about to come true. She'd make it in under seventeen hours even if she had to crawl the rest of the way.

Brian, however, had started ten minutes earlier than she had. He didn't have a second to spare. He might DNF, finishing only a few agonizing seconds too late. Sheila knew she couldn't slow down and run beside him. When she'd tried that, it had backfired. Instead, she had to pull him home with the invisible, emotional cord of whatever had developed between them.

She rounded the corner into the finishing chute, the crowds three deep behind metal police barriers and cheering loudly, the PA announcer giving the cherished words to runner after runner, "You are an Ironman!"

Sheila longed to hear those words, and knew she soon would. She also wanted to high-five all the total strangers lining the chute and share her victory. But there would be no high-fiving.

She had to get Brian across the finish line in time. *Had to!* Sheila glanced over her shoulder, yelled, "You can do it!" and thought of a way to help him at the very end.

Even with his mind ablur, scarcely able to add two plus two, Brian knew he had started with 19:38 on the clock, nineteen minutes and thirty-eight seconds after the elites. It was etched in his brain. He needed to finish before the clock above the finish line read 17:19:38.

He entered the chute to the finish line, every muscle screaming in agony, eyes fixed to the back of Sheila's neon top. *Follow Sheila home!* He barely heard the crowd cheering, the noisemakers blaring, and the PA announcer.

He only saw Sheila. And then the clock above the finish line: 17:18:09.

He had barely a minute left—assuming his clouded brain was working well enough to calculate it correctly— with the longest hundred yards in his life remaining.

Follow Sheila home!

17:18:45.

Brian's legs wobbled like rubber, but he kept his eyes pinned on Sheila. Kept his legs moving.

Follow Sheila!

17:19:00.

As she crossed the finish line, the Public Address announcer proclaimed, "Sheila Watkins, you are an Ironman!"

Smiling ear-to-ear, Sheila turned to welcome him with open arms.

"*Go!*" Sheila hollered, arms wide, knowing she'd burst into tears if he didn't make it. "*Go!*"

Ten yards left. 17:19:20.

"*Go!*"

Five left.

"*Go!!!*"

Brian crossed the finish line, and the PA announcer boomed, "Brian O'Connell, you are an Ironman!"

17:19:27! Made it by eleven seconds!

Brian all but collapsed into Sheila's arms. She wrapped her arms around him and hugged him tight, and he hugged her. She wasn't sure which one of them smelled worse, but it didn't matter.

"We did it!" they cried in unison, clinging to each other until a short, blond-haired woman draped silver foil, thermal blankets over their shoulders and asked them to move down the chute to clear the finish line.

"I couldn't have done it without you," Brian said when they reached the metal police barriers at the end of the chute. They embraced again, their grime-covered, sweat-caked faces just inches apart. "What can I ever do to repay you?"

Sheila gazed into his green eyes. "Get me some Cape Cod chips. But first, if you're interested, give me a kiss."

Brian smiled. "More interested than you can know."

With their arms wrapped tightly around each other, they kissed. Even though their dry, salty lips were chapped, their hair tangled, and their sweaty aroma would never be featured in a perfume or cologne, none of that mattered.

The kiss was long and lovely, and she knew it was just the first of many more to come.

Thank you for your interest in my books.

D H H

Newsletter

Also by David H. Hendrickson

Novels: Romance

Body Check

No Defense

Romantic Concerto for Strings and Brass

Novels: Young Adult/Sports/Historical

Cracking the Ice

Offside

Offensive Foul

Bottom of the Ninth

The Rabbit Labelle Trilogy (Omnibus)

Novels: Humor/Crime

Bubba Goes for Broke

Novels: Mystery/Suspense

Pain Train (forthcoming)

Collections

Shimmers and Laughs: Eight Wildly Hilarious Tales

Death in the Serengeti and Other Stories: Ten Tales of Crime

The Boy in the Boxers and Other Stories of Sweet Romance

Hell of a Band: Twelve Fantasy Stories

Fighting the Dying Light: Stories of Aging (forthcoming)

Cape Cod Chips, Wiener Dogs, and Swiping Left: Stories of Sweet Romance (forthcoming)

The Soulmate Junkie and Other Stories of Fantasy & Science Fiction (forthcoming)

Crime From Another Time: Stories of Mystery and Suspense (forthcoming)

Crime Fantastique: Stories of Mystery and Suspense (forthcoming)

Crime, Up Close and Personal: Stories of Mystery and Suspense (forthcoming)

Nonfiction

How to Get Your Book Into Schools and Double Your Income With Volume Sales

Travis Roy: Quadriplegia and a Life of Purpose

Hendu's Story: From Dream to Reality

Acknowledgments

To Dean Wesley Smith and Annie Reed, the editors who believed in these stories.

To Annie Reed, also the editor of this collection, whose expertise I can always rely on.

To my readers, whose enthusiasm helps keep me going.

To all my family and friends, who support me during the valleys and celebrate with me on the mountaintops.

About the Author

David H. Hendrickson's first novel, *Cracking the Ice*, was praised by *Booklist* as "a gripping account of a courageous young man rising above evil." He has since published seven additional novels, including *Offside*, which has been adopted for high school student required reading.

His short fiction has appeared in *Best American Mystery Stories 2018*, *Ellery Queen's Mystery Magazine*, *Thrill Ride - the Magazine*, *Heart's Kiss*, almost every issue of *Pulphouse Fiction Magazine* and *Mystery, Crime, and Mayhem*, as well as numerous anthologies, including over a half dozen issues of *Fiction River*. He is a multi-finalist for the Derringer Award, and his story "Death in the Serengeti" was honored with the 2018 Derringer Award for Best Long Story.

He has published five short story collections with five more forthcoming. Currently available: *Shimmers and Laughs: Eight Wildly Hilarious Tales*; *Death in the Serengeti and Other Stories: Ten Tales of Crime*; *The Boy in the Boxers and Other Stories of Sweet Romance*; *Hell of a Band: Twelve Fantasy Stories*; and *Fighting the Dying Light: Stories of Aging*.

Hendrickson has published over fifteen hundred works of nonfiction, most notably his first book for writers, *How to Get Your Book into Schools and Double Your Income with*

Volume Sales, and also *Travis Roy: Quadriplegia and a Life of Purpose* and *Hendu's Story: From Dream to Reality*. He has been honored with the Joe Concannon Hockey East Media Award and the Murray Kramer Scarlet Quill Award.

Visit him online at www.hendricksonwriter.com.